The Everyday Trader - Trader's Fight for Success

Anshumala Singh

Published by Anshumala Singh, 2024.

THE EVERYDAY TRADER - TRADER'S FIGHT FOR SUCCESS

First edition. October 3, 2024.

Copyright © 2024 Anshumala Singh.

ISBN: 979-8227266651

Written by Anshumala Singh.

The Everyday Trader - Trader's Fight for Success

Dear Reader,

Welcome to **"The Everyday Trader - Trader's Fight for Success,"** a story that dives deep into the heart of the modern trader's journey. This book isn't just about the numbers and charts that dominate financial markets—it's about the emotions, challenges, and resilience required to navigate this unpredictable world.

Aarya's journey mirrors the experiences of so many individuals who have ventured into the stock market, driven by dreams of financial freedom and success. In the beginning, it all seems so simple—the promise of quick profits and the allure of mastering the market. But as Aarya quickly learns, the reality is far more complex and demanding. His story reflects the highs and lows that come with trading: the thrill of early success, the devastation of unexpected losses, and the temptation to take that one big risk in pursuit of a windfall.

Through this book, I hope to shine a light on the emotional rollercoaster that everyday traders experience. It's not just about making money; it's about understanding yourself, managing risks, learning from mistakes, and ultimately fighting to stay in the game. The stock market, like life, can be both exhilarating and unforgiving. It tests our patience, challenges our discipline, and pushes us to face our fears head-on.

I've written this story not only to entertain but to offer a deeper perspective into the psychology of trading. The character of Aarya could be anyone—anyone who has dreamed of something more, taken bold risks, faced setbacks, and found the strength to rise again. It's a story of perseverance, grit, and growth, and I hope it resonates with anyone who has faced challenges in their own financial journey.

Thank you for joining me on this adventure. Whether you're a seasoned trader or just someone curious about the stock market, I believe Aarya's story will inspire you to keep pushing forward, even when the odds seem stacked against you.

Wishing you success in all your ventures,

Anshumala Singh

Author of *The Everyday Trader - Trader's Fight for Success*

Preface

The world of trading is like no other. It's a battlefield where decisions made in mere seconds can lead to either glorious triumph or devastating defeat. For those on the outside, the stock market often appears to be a place where money flows effortlessly, where people simply click a button and watch their fortunes rise. But for those who have walked the trader's path, the reality is far different—it's a journey filled with uncertainty, anxiety, victories, and heartbreaks.

"The Everyday Trader - Trader's Fight for Success" is a story inspired by these very highs and lows, reflecting the experiences of countless traders who risk it all to chase their dreams. This book isn't a guide on how to trade or a technical manual on market strategies. Instead, it's an exploration of the human side of trading—the emotions, the psychological battles, and the immense pressure that come with trying to outsmart the market.

Through the eyes of Aarya, our protagonist, you'll witness the rollercoaster journey of an everyday trader: the early optimism, the crushing losses, the moments of doubt, and the relentless desire to succeed. The story reveals the risks people take, the traps they fall into, and the perseverance it takes to stay in the game.

My goal with this book is to connect with anyone who has ever taken a financial risk or dreamed of achieving something big, only to realize the path is fraught with unexpected challenges. This book is a tribute to the resilience of the human spirit, and I hope it will inspire and resonate with you as you read.

Introduction

In the fast-paced world of financial markets, fortunes can be made and lost in the blink of an eye. But what drives people to enter this unpredictable game in the first place? For many, it's the allure of freedom—the chance to escape the constraints of a regular job, to control their own destiny, and to unlock the potential for financial independence. But behind every trade, every calculated risk, there's a deeper story.

Aarya, the protagonist of this story, represents that everyman trader. He is not an institutional investor with millions at his disposal, nor is he backed by teams of analysts and algorithms. He is simply a dreamer, like many of us, looking for a way to make his mark in the world. Aarya's journey begins with high hopes, encouraged by early wins that spark his passion for the stock market. But as the chapters unfold, he soon learns that trading is not just about reading charts and spotting trends. It's about managing emotions, taking calculated risks, and, most importantly, surviving the inevitable setbacks.

In the stock market, success is never guaranteed. There are traps along the way—like the allure of margin trading, the temptation to "go all in" on a hot tip, or the false confidence that early wins can create. Through Aarya's experiences, this story explores these very traps and the lessons they teach.

This book is for the everyday trader—the one who trades from a laptop in their living room, who stays up late researching stocks, and who dreams of that one big win. It's for those who have tasted both victory and defeat in the market, and who continue to fight for success. Aarya's journey reflects the realities of trading: it's a battle not just against the market, but against oneself.

As you read, you'll see how Aarya navigates this world of uncertainty, how he learns to cope with loss, and how he ultimately fights for his place in the market. The story is a reminder that success doesn't come easy, but with perseverance, it is possible.

Welcome to the journey of **The Everyday Trader**—a tale of ambition, risk, failure, and triumph.

Chapter 15: The Everyday Legend

Chapter 1: Dreams in the Dust

Aarya sat at his desk, staring at the flickering screen of his office computer, but his mind was far away from the spreadsheets and reports that filled his day. The soft hum of the air conditioner, the distant clatter of keyboards, and the monotonous routine that had become his life felt like a cage—one he had willingly stepped into years ago when he first took up his job. But now, after years of staring at the same grey walls, following the same routine, he could no longer shake the feeling that he was wasting his life away.

Aarya, like many of his colleagues, was a middle-class worker. He lived in a small but comfortable flat in a bustling city, just enough to get by but not enough to satisfy his growing hunger for something more. Every morning, he woke up, traveled the same route to the office, sat in the same cubicle, and worked on tasks that seemed to blur together, day after day. He was good at his job—efficient, punctual, and reliable—but the spark of enthusiasm he once had had long since fizzled out. The days stretched on, each one blending into the next, a cycle of monotony he felt powerless to break.

But something had changed in Aarya. Lately, he had been hearing stories—stories of ordinary people like him who had broken free from the 9-to-5 grind and found financial freedom in the most unlikely of places: the stock market. He had heard of people making fortunes overnight, turning small investments into life-changing sums of money. The stories fueled his imagination, igniting a spark of hope deep within him. He began to see the stock market as his way out, a ticket to a life free from the constraints of his job and the ever-looming shadow of financial limitations.

At first, Aarya dismissed the idea as a pipe dream. How could he, a man with no background in finance, navigate the complex world of stocks, trades, and investments? But the more he thought about it, the more plausible it seemed. The internet was filled with articles, videos, and courses that promised to teach people how to trade. And didn't the success stories prove that it was possible? If others could do it, why not him?

One evening, after yet another long, tiring day at work, Aarya found himself sitting in front of his computer, typing "how to start trading stocks" into the search bar. As the results flooded in, he was overwhelmed by the sheer amount of information available. There were articles detailing the basics of stock trading, YouTube videos of successful traders sharing their strategies, and countless platforms offering courses on the subject. The more he read, the more his interest grew. He learned about stock indices, the concept of buying low and selling high, and the potential for substantial gains through short-term trading.

But what truly caught Aarya's attention was the allure of day trading—buying and selling stocks within the same day to capitalize on small price movements. The idea that he could make money quickly, without waiting years for investments to grow, was intoxicating. The thrill of potentially earning more in a day than he could in a month at his job made his heart race. It was risky, he knew, but the potential rewards seemed worth it.

Over the next few weeks, Aarya threw himself into studying the market. In his spare time—during lunch breaks, late at night, and even on weekends—he devoured information on stocks, trading strategies, and market trends. He began to understand the language of the market: candlestick charts, moving averages, support and resistance levels. Terms that once seemed foreign to him now started to make sense.

His initial research only deepened his belief that the stock market was his key to freedom. He envisioned himself quitting his job, traveling the world, and living life on his own terms, all while earning money from his laptop. He imagined walking into his boss's office, handing in his resignation, and leaving the corporate world behind. It felt liberating just to think about it.

But alongside the excitement, there was a growing sense of unease. Aarya was a cautious man by nature, and the idea of risking his hard-earned money on something as unpredictable as the stock market was terrifying. What if he lost it all? What if he made a bad decision and wiped out his savings? These thoughts gnawed at him, but they were drowned out by the louder, more insistent voice that kept whispering in his ear: "What if you succeed?"

The stories of others who had made it big kept playing in his mind. He read about a man who had turned a modest investment into millions through savvy trades, and another who had quit his corporate job to trade full-time and never looked back. Aarya found himself daydreaming about joining their ranks, imagining himself in the same position—successful, wealthy, free. The more he thought about it, the more determined he became to take the plunge.

One night, as he sat on his couch with his laptop, Aarya made a decision. He was going to start trading. He wasn't sure where the journey would take him, but he knew one thing: he couldn't continue living the way he was. The thought of spending the next 20 or 30 years working the same job, living paycheck to paycheck, filled him with dread. Trading offered a way out, a chance to break free from the cycle of mediocrity and chase something bigger.

But Aarya knew that if he was going to succeed, he needed to be prepared. He wasn't about to dive headfirst into the market without a plan. Over the next few days, he created a strategy. He decided to start small, using a portion of his savings to test the waters. He would trade cautiously at first, learning the ropes before risking larger amounts of money. It was a plan that made sense, and it gave him the confidence to move forward.

Aarya's first foray into the stock market was exciting and nerve-wracking. He opened a trading account, carefully selected a few stocks, and made his first trades. The rush of adrenaline he felt as he watched the prices fluctuate was unlike anything he had experienced before. It was exhilarating, but also terrifying. Every decision felt weighty, every movement of the market fraught with potential consequences.

In those early days, Aarya had both wins and losses. His first few trades were small, but they gave him a taste of the market's potential. When he made a profit, no matter how modest, he felt a surge of confidence. But the losses, though not catastrophic, were sobering. It became clear to him that this was not going to be easy. The stock market was unpredictable, and no amount of research could guarantee success.

Despite the setbacks, Aarya's enthusiasm didn't wane. If anything, the losses only made him more determined to succeed. He saw them as learning experiences, opportunities to improve his strategy and sharpen his instincts. He began to understand that trading was not just about reading charts and analyzing data—it was about managing emotions, controlling fear and greed, and staying disciplined in the face of uncertainty.

As Aarya delved deeper into the world of trading, he started to notice changes in himself. He became more focused, more determined. The stock market consumed his thoughts, even when he wasn't actively trading. He found himself thinking about it during meetings at work, while commuting, and even when spending time with friends and family. Trading had become more than just a hobby—it was an obsession.

But with obsession came isolation. Aarya's friends and colleagues couldn't understand why he was so consumed by the stock market. To them, it seemed like a reckless gamble, a foolish pursuit of wealth that would likely end in disappointment. They warned him about the risks, about the countless people who had lost everything trying to beat the market. But Aarya brushed off their concerns. He was different, he told himself. He was careful, calculated. He wasn't about to throw away his future on a whim.

Still, the doubts lingered in the back of his mind. Was he really making the right choice? Was this all just a fantasy, a desperate attempt to escape the realities of his life? Aarya didn't know for sure, but one thing was certain: he couldn't go back to the way things were. The life he had been living, the safe, predictable existence he had once found comfort in, now felt like a prison. Trading was his way out, and he was willing to take the risk.

As the days turned into weeks, Aarya's confidence grew. He was still cautious, but with each trade, he felt like he was getting closer to his goal. The small wins he accumulated were enough to keep him going, fueling his belief that financial freedom was within his grasp. But deep down, Aarya knew that the road ahead was fraught with challenges. The stock market was a dangerous game, and success was never guaranteed.

Yet, despite the risks, despite the uncertainty, Aarya couldn't shake the feeling that this was what he was meant to do. Trading wasn't just about money—it was about taking control of his life, about breaking free from the constraints that had held him back for so long. It was about chasing a dream, even if that dream seemed impossible.

And so, with a heart full of hope and a mind filled with doubt, Aarya embarked on his journey into the world of trading, not knowing where it would lead, but certain that he could never turn back.

Chapter 2: The Beginner's Charm

Aarya could hardly believe his eyes as he stared at the numbers on his screen. The stock price had surged, and his small, cautious investment had turned a tidy profit in just a matter of hours. His heart raced, and a wave of excitement washed over him. This was it—the moment he had been dreaming about for months. The stock market, which had seemed so intimidating just weeks ago, now felt like a gold mine that he had begun to unlock. For the first time in a long while, Aarya felt like he was in control of his destiny.

It had taken months of late nights and early mornings, poring over charts, financial reports, and trading tutorials, but Aarya had finally made his first trade. He'd been nervous, of course—placing his hard-earned money into the hands of an unpredictable market was no small step. Yet, despite the anxiety that had gripped him as he clicked the "buy" button, it had been immediately followed by the intoxicating thrill of watching the stock price creep upwards, and then surge. The small gain he made wasn't life-changing, but it was enough to set his mind racing with possibilities.

"I can do this," he thought, a sense of pride swelling inside him. The numbers in his account had grown, and with them, his confidence. He felt as though he had cracked some hidden code, stumbled upon a secret that only a few knew. Maybe he had a natural talent for this, a gift for reading the market that others didn't possess.

The next few days passed in a blur of exhilaration. Aarya couldn't stop replaying the trade in his head, the rush of making the right decision at the right time. It felt like a victory—a validation of all the time and effort he had put into learning the intricacies of trading. He had watched videos, read books, and studied market trends with an almost obsessive dedication, and now, it seemed to be paying off. He had always been diligent and meticulous in his approach to work, and he believed those qualities had given him an edge in trading as well.

Yet, despite the excitement, there was a quiet voice in the back of his mind whispering caution. He had read countless stories of traders who had experienced early success, only to see it all evaporate in an instant. He reminded himself that the stock market was volatile and unpredictable, and that one good trade didn't guarantee future success. Still, it was hard to resist the temptation to celebrate. He had made money—real money—and it had been quick and easy. The thrill of that first win was addictive, and Aarya found himself already thinking about his next trade.

In the days following his initial success, Aarya dove even deeper into the world of trading. He scoured financial news websites, followed market analysts on social media, and kept a close eye on his trading platform, watching the prices of various stocks fluctuate throughout the day. The more he immersed himself in the market, the more confident he became that this was something he could excel at.

But there was also an undercurrent of impatience brewing within him. The success of his first trade had made him hungry for more, and the slow, deliberate approach he had initially planned now seemed too cautious. Aarya began to think that maybe he was being overly conservative. After all, his first trade had been a success—why shouldn't the next one be as well?

The stock market was like a living, breathing entity to him now, one that ebbed and flowed with each passing minute. He was learning to read its rhythms, to sense when the time was right to buy or sell. At least, that's what he told himself. With each passing day, the excitement of trading grew, but so did the pressure. He wanted to replicate the success of his first trade, to prove that it wasn't just a fluke.

It wasn't long before Aarya made his second trade. This time, he invested a little more than before. The confidence he had gained from his first win had emboldened him, and he felt ready to take on a bit more risk. The stock he chose seemed like a sure bet—it had been steadily climbing for days, and the company's financials looked solid. Aarya was certain that this trade would bring him another quick profit.

And it did.

Once again, the stock rose shortly after he bought it, and within a few hours, Aarya had made another profit. This one was slightly larger than the first, and the sense of accomplishment he felt was even stronger. He had done it again—two trades, two wins. The excitement he felt was almost overwhelming. He was starting to believe that he really did have a knack for this, that he was on his way to becoming a successful trader.

But as Aarya's confidence grew, so did his blind spots. He started to overlook the role of luck in his early wins, attributing his success solely to his skill and instincts. He didn't notice that the broader market had been on an upswing during his trades, making it easier for even novice traders to profit. Instead, Aarya began to see himself as someone who could consistently beat the market, someone who had the ability to read the signals that others missed.

With each success, Aarya felt the intoxicating pull of the stock market tighten its grip on him. The thrill of watching a stock rise, the rush of making a profit—it was becoming an addiction. He began to fantasize about what his life could look like if he continued on this path. He imagined quitting his job, becoming a full-time trader, and living a life of financial independence. The idea of making money from the comfort of his own home, without the constraints of a traditional job, was incredibly appealing. It seemed like a dream come true, and Aarya was more determined than ever to make it a reality.

But the more Aarya traded, the more he started to push his limits. He began to take on riskier trades, convinced that his early success was a sign that he had a natural gift for the market. He no longer saw the need to play it safe—after all, he had already proven that he could make money through trading. He started to invest larger amounts, taking on positions in more volatile stocks, all the while believing that he could handle the risks.

And for a while, it seemed to work. Aarya continued to make small profits, and each one reinforced his belief that he was on the right track.

The stock market, which had once seemed so daunting, now felt like a game—a game that he was winning. But what Aarya didn't realize was that the market's upswing wouldn't last forever. The volatility that had worked in his favor so far could just as easily turn against him.

It wasn't long before Aarya encountered his first real loss. He had invested in a stock that had shown promising signs of growth, but instead of rising, it plummeted. In a matter of hours, Aarya watched helplessly as the value of his investment dropped, erasing a significant portion of his gains from previous trades. His stomach churned as he stared at the screen, unable to believe what he was seeing. For the first time since he had started trading, he felt a deep sense of panic.

Aarya had known, intellectually, that losses were a part of trading. He had read about it, and he had even prepared himself for the possibility. But knowing it and experiencing it were two very different things. The reality of watching his money disappear was gut-wrenching, and Aarya realized that the stock market wasn't as easy as he had thought. His early wins had given him a false sense of security, and now, that illusion was starting to crumble.

The loss shook Aarya's confidence. For the first time, he questioned whether he had made the right decision by getting involved in trading. Maybe his friends and colleagues had been right to warn him about the risks. Maybe he had been too naive, too eager to believe that he could make a living from the stock market. The doubts that he had pushed aside were now flooding back, and Aarya found himself wondering if he was in over his head.

But even as the doubts crept in, Aarya couldn't shake the desire to keep going. The stock market had become more than just a way to make money—it had become a challenge, a test of his skills and determination. He wasn't ready to give up, not yet. The thrill of his early wins still lingered in his mind, and he couldn't resist the urge to try again, to prove to himself that he could bounce back from this setback.

In the days that followed, Aarya threw himself back into studying the market. He analyzed his past trades, trying to understand what had gone wrong and how he could avoid making the same mistake in the future. He watched videos, read articles, and sought advice from experienced traders online. Aarya was determined to learn from his loss, to use it as a stepping stone to future success.

But deep down, Aarya knew that the stock market was unpredictable. No amount of research or preparation could guarantee success, and he would have to learn to live with the uncertainty. Yet, despite the risks, Aarya couldn't resist the allure of the market. The promise of financial freedom, the thrill of making a successful trade, the challenge of navigating the complexities of the market—it was all too enticing.

As Aarya prepared for his next trade, he knew that the journey ahead would be filled with highs and lows. There would be wins and losses, moments of triumph and moments of doubt. But one thing was certain: Aarya was in it for the long haul. He had tasted the thrill of success, and he wasn't ready to walk away. The stock market had become a part of him now, and he was determined to see where the journey would take him.

Chapter 3: Walking on Thin Ice

The morning sun filtered through the curtains of Aarya's small apartment, casting a soft glow on his face. His laptop screen was already open, displaying the latest stock market trends, but Aarya wasn't paying attention to the numbers just yet. Instead, his mind was racing, fuelled by the heady mix of excitement and anticipation. His early successes had filled him with a sense of power, and as he sat there sipping his morning coffee, Aarya couldn't help but feel like he was on the brink of something much bigger.

He had come far from those tentative first steps in the world of stock trading. What had begun as a hobby, something he explored during his spare time, had now turned into a near obsession. His modest gains had given him a rush of confidence, a belief that he had the natural instincts of a successful trader. His wins felt like validation of his potential, and the lure of bigger rewards was impossible to ignore.

Aarya's gaze shifted to the screen, where a discussion on one of his favorite trading forums had caught his eye. The post was from a self-proclaimed expert, boasting about an "undervalued gem" in the market. The comments section was ablaze with enthusiastic traders, all of whom claimed they were getting in on the opportunity.

He had seen this kind of excitement before—traders rallying around a stock based on tips and promises of quick riches. It was the sort of hype that made the stock seem like a sure bet. Aarya had always been cautious about these recommendations, relying instead on his own research, but now, with a string of profitable trades behind him, he felt more emboldened. Maybe this time, the collective wisdom of the trading community had struck gold.

He hovered his mouse over the stock ticker, checking the company's financials briefly. It was a small, relatively unknown company, but the numbers looked decent enough, and the buzz around it was undeniable.

"Should I go for it?" he muttered to himself, the weight of the decision pressing on his mind. His recent successes had made him more comfortable with risk, and the more he thought about it, the more he rationalized that this could be his chance to accelerate his gains.

Just a few months ago, Aarya would have hesitated, analyzing every possible outcome before making a decision. But now, with confidence built on the back of his early wins, he clicked "buy," placing a larger-than-usual portion of his savings into the stock. It was a bold move—bolder than anything he had attempted so far—but Aarya had convinced himself that it was the right one.

Days passed, and the stock began to rise, just as the online forums had predicted. Aarya watched with growing satisfaction as his account balance inched upward, reaffirming his belief that he was on the right track. It was a small win, but it felt significant. The adrenaline rush that came with watching the stock rise was intoxicating, and with each small success, Aarya's appetite for more grew stronger.

But something else was growing too—his willingness to take risks.

The more Aarya traded, the more he found himself relying on the advice of strangers from online forums and social media influencers. These self-proclaimed experts painted vivid pictures of market trends and upcoming booms, and Aarya began to find their advice comforting. He told himself that they had more experience, more insight into the market, and that their success stories were proof of their credibility.

It wasn't long before Aarya started following these tips more frequently, often buying into stocks without doing much of his own research. He rationalized it by saying that he was simply leveraging the collective knowledge of the community, but deep down, he knew that he was cutting corners. The thrill of making quick profits was clouding his judgment, and Aarya was walking on increasingly thin ice.

One evening, after a particularly exhausting day at work, Aarya slouched on his couch, his laptop perched precariously on his lap. The markets were still open, and he was scrolling through the same online forums, seeking out the next big tip. His recent trades had been a mix of wins and losses, but he hadn't suffered anything catastrophic yet.

However, he couldn't shake the feeling that something was missing—his strategy, once solid and methodical, now felt haphazard. His success had been sporadic, and each win seemed more like a stroke of luck than a result of careful planning. The stock market was becoming more volatile, and while some of the tips he followed worked out, others had left him frustrated and nursing small losses.

But it was a post on the forum that caught his attention that night—a stock trading at a "bargain price," with promises of doubling in value within weeks. The excitement in the thread was palpable, with traders chiming in from every corner, encouraging others to get in while they could. Aarya felt that familiar rush of excitement and temptation. He had the funds to invest, and though the stock was risky, the potential rewards seemed too good to pass up.

"This could be it," he thought. "This could be the one that makes up for all the small losses."

The allure of making a quick profit was overpowering. Aarya clicked on the stock, analyzed the price charts for a few minutes—far less time than he would have spent months ago—and made his decision. He bought in, this time committing a substantial portion of his capital. He convinced himself that the experts in the forum knew what they were talking about, that this was an opportunity he couldn't afford to miss.

The days that followed were tense. Aarya watched the stock price closely, refreshing the page every few minutes, hoping for a sign that he had made the right decision. But instead of rising, the stock began to fluctuate wildly. It would go up a little, giving him a brief glimmer of hope, only to plunge down again, erasing whatever gains it had made.

At first, Aarya tried to stay calm, telling himself that the market was just experiencing normal volatility. But as the stock continued its erratic behavior, his confidence began to waver. The experts in the forum had assured everyone that this was a temporary dip, that the stock would bounce back any day now. But Aarya wasn't so sure.

His account balance was shrinking, and with it, his faith in the advice he had followed. He had been here before—on the edge of a significant loss—and it was a feeling he didn't want to experience again. But this time, the stakes were higher. Aarya had invested more than he could afford to lose, and the realization hit him like a ton of bricks.

Panic began to set in.

He spent hours scouring the internet for news about the company, looking for any indication that the stock would recover. But the more he searched, the more uncertain he became. The hype from the online forums had died down, and many of the so-called experts had gone silent. The stock was sinking fast, and Aarya knew that if he didn't act soon, he could lose everything.

One morning, Aarya woke up to find that the stock had taken another dive, this time a sharp one. His heart sank as he stared at the screen, the numbers flashing in red. He was now sitting on a significant loss, and the fear of losing even more gripped him.

For the first time in his trading journey, Aarya felt completely out of control. The confidence that had carried him through his early successes had vanished, replaced by a deep sense of regret. He had let himself get swept up in the excitement of easy money, and now, he was paying the price.

In that moment of clarity, Aarya made the painful decision to sell. It was a hard blow, watching his investment evaporate in an instant, but he knew it was the right move. The stock was too volatile, too unpredictable, and he couldn't afford to risk any more. He closed his laptop with a heavy heart, the weight of his loss pressing down on him.

That night, Aarya lay in bed, staring at the ceiling. The thrill of the stock market, the excitement of making money, had faded, leaving behind a bitter aftertaste. He had been reckless, blinded by his early successes and seduced by the allure of quick wealth. The risks he had taken, once manageable, had grown too large, and now he was paying the price.

But even as the sting of his loss lingered, Aarya couldn't help but feel a flicker of hope. He had made mistakes—big ones—but he had also learned valuable lessons. The stock market wasn't just a game of chance; it required patience, discipline, and a clear strategy. And though he had stumbled, Aarya knew that he still had the potential to succeed.

As he drifted off to sleep, Aarya resolved to approach the market differently. He would no longer rely on the advice of strangers or chase after the promise of easy money. From now on, he would focus on building a strategy that was his own—one grounded in careful analysis, not hype.

It was a hard lesson to learn, but Aarya knew that he was stronger for it. The ice may have cracked beneath him, but he hadn't fallen through just yet.

Chapter 4: Shattered Illusions

Aarya sat motionless, staring at his laptop screen. His heart pounded in his chest, his hands trembled, and a cold sweat broke out on his forehead. The blinking red numbers on the trading dashboard told him everything he didn't want to believe. It wasn't just a bad day in the market—this was catastrophic. His mind raced, trying to make sense of what had happened, but no amount of rationalization could undo the damage. In a matter of hours, most of his capital had been wiped out.

This wasn't supposed to happen, Aarya thought. He had followed the strategies he had learned, trusted the expert opinions he had relied on, and made the decisions he believed would lead him to success. Yet, here he was, confronting a loss so significant it left him feeling physically sick. His stomach churned, and he had to swallow hard to keep himself from throwing up.

For the past few months, Aarya's trading journey had felt like a steady rise to glory. His early wins had inflated his confidence, leading him to believe he had a natural talent for stock trading. With every small success, he had grown bolder, taking larger risks and ignoring the warning signs that he wasn't nearly as prepared as he thought. He had been walking on thin ice, and now, with this massive loss, that ice had finally shattered beneath him.

The day had started like any other. Aarya woke up early, as he usually did, eager to check the markets and make his next move. He had a morning routine—check the forums for tips, review his portfolio, and decide whether to hold or sell his positions. The stock he had recently invested in, based on glowing recommendations from the online community, had been fluctuating for days, but he had held firm, convinced it was just temporary volatility.

He remembered the feeling of hope when he logged in that morning. The stock had dipped slightly, but nothing too concerning. Aarya believed in the company's potential, having convinced himself that the rumors of its impending growth were true. As he sat at his desk, sipping his coffee, he felt calm, almost confident that things would turn around.

But by mid-morning, everything changed.

The stock price started to drop rapidly. At first, Aarya remained optimistic—this was the nature of the market, after all. Stocks went up and down all the time, and he had seen dips like this before. But as the minutes ticked by, the dip turned into a nosedive. The price plummeted, faster than he could have ever imagined. The small losses that had once seemed insignificant quickly turned into a massive black hole, swallowing up his capital.

Aarya frantically refreshed the page, hoping against hope that this was just a glitch or a temporary market fluctuation. But it wasn't. The company had announced unexpected financial troubles, and the stock was collapsing in real-time. He watched in horror as his balance drained away, helpless to stop it. He had placed too much trust in the stock, too much of his money, and now he was paying the price.

By the time he realized what was happening, it was too late. The losses were too deep to recover from, and selling now would only lock in the disaster. But doing nothing meant watching his account dwindle further. It was a no-win situation. Aarya sat frozen, his mind paralyzed by fear and regret.

The emotional toll hit him harder than the financial one. He had always prided himself on being level-headed, able to handle stress without letting it overwhelm him. But this loss was different. This was personal. It wasn't just about the money—it was about the dreams he had attached to that money. Every trade, every investment, had been a step toward a future he had envisioned for himself—a future of financial freedom, of escaping the grind of his mundane office job, of becoming someone who could provide for his family without worry.

But now, in the blink of an eye, those dreams felt shattered. The weight of his failure pressed down on him like a ton of bricks, suffocating him. He replayed every decision in his mind, questioning where he had gone wrong. How could he have been so foolish? How could he have let himself get swept up in the excitement of easy money? He had been warned, hadn't he? The forums, the articles—everyone had said that trading was risky, that the market could turn against you in an instant. But Aarya hadn't listened. He had believed he was different, that he had what it took to beat the odds.

The realization that he had been wrong, that he wasn't as smart or as skilled as he had thought, was crushing.

For the next few days, Aarya avoided his trading account altogether. He couldn't bear to look at the numbers, the glaring reminder of his failure. He stopped reading the forums, stopped checking the market news—everything that had once excited him now filled him with dread. The joy of trading, the thrill of making money, had been replaced by a deep sense of loss and regret.

At night, he would lie awake in bed, his mind consumed with thoughts of what could have been. He imagined a different version of himself—the version that had made the right decisions, the version that had sold at the right time and walked away with a profit. That version of Aarya was living the life he had dreamed of, while the real Aarya was left to pick up the pieces of his shattered illusions.

The loss had shaken him to his core, and for the first time since he had started trading, Aarya questioned whether he had made a terrible mistake by entering this world. Maybe he wasn't cut out for it. Maybe the stock market was too ruthless, too unpredictable, for someone like him.

But giving up wasn't an option. He couldn't just walk away, not after everything he had invested—both financially and emotionally. He had put too much on the line to quit now. And besides, the loss, as devastating as it was, hadn't wiped him out completely. There was still a chance, a small one, to rebuild.

The next week, Aarya forced himself to sit down at his computer and log back into his trading account. His balance was a shadow of what it had once been, but he hadn't lost everything. He took a deep breath, his hands shaking as he navigated the site. He needed to regroup, to come up with a new plan. But how? The strategies he had relied on before had failed him. The advice from the forums had led him astray.

Aarya realized that he had been trading blindly, relying on the opinions of others instead of doing his own research. He had gotten swept up in the hype, convinced that every stock tip was a golden opportunity. But the market didn't work that way. It wasn't a get-rich-quick scheme—it was a battlefield, and he had been woefully unprepared.

The loss had been a wake-up call, a harsh reminder that success in the stock market wasn't about luck or following the crowd. It required discipline, strategy, and most importantly, a deep understanding of the risks involved.

As Aarya stared at his diminished balance, he knew that he had two choices: he could either walk away, chalking up the entire experience as a painful lesson, or he could double down, learn from his mistakes, and try again.

Walking away would have been the easier option. It would have spared him the stress, the anxiety, and the emotional rollercoaster that came with trading. But Aarya wasn't ready to quit. Deep down, he knew that he still had the potential to succeed, but it would require a complete overhaul of his approach. He couldn't afford to make the same mistakes again.

From now on, Aarya vowed to rely on his own analysis, to trust his instincts rather than the noise from the forums. He would build a solid foundation of knowledge, studying the market trends and learning the technical aspects of trading that he had previously ignored. This time, he would be prepared.

But even as he made this vow, Aarya couldn't shake the feeling of fear that lingered in the back of his mind. The stock market had shown him its ruthless side, and he knew that if he wasn't careful, it could crush him again.

The illusion of easy success had been shattered, and in its place was the harsh reality of the trading world. It was a world that could offer incredible rewards, but only to those who were willing to face its challenges head-on.

Aarya was determined to be one of those people, but as he sat there, staring at his screen, he couldn't help but wonder—how much more would he have to lose before he finally won?

Chapter 5: Borrowed Time

Aarya sat at his desk, staring at the spreadsheets he had meticulously created to track his trades. The numbers were cold, indifferent reminders of his mistakes. His once-growing portfolio was now a shell of what it had been, and despite his best efforts to come up with a new strategy, he couldn't shake the overwhelming sense of dread that crept into his mind whenever he thought about the future. The loss he had taken in the last chapter of his life still weighed heavily on him, gnawing at his confidence, whispering doubts into his ears.

But it wasn't just about the loss anymore. It was about something deeper—the dream he had nurtured for months, the dream of breaking free from the monotonous grind of his job and achieving financial independence. That dream felt farther away than ever, almost unattainable. And yet, he couldn't let go. He couldn't walk away from the trading world that had promised him so much, even if it had so far delivered only disappointment.

That's when the idea first struck him—borrowing money.

At first, it seemed like a lifeline, a way to climb out of the pit he had dug for himself. With more capital to trade, he reasoned, he could bounce back. The market couldn't stay down forever. A few well-placed trades, and he would not only recover his losses but also make a profit. It wasn't just wishful thinking, he told himself. It was part of the plan. He had learned from his mistakes, hadn't he? He was smarter now, more cautious. This time, things would be different.

The conversation with the bank was surprisingly easy. Aarya had been a loyal customer for years, and his credit score was strong—at least, it had been before he'd taken those big losses. The loan officer barely asked any questions. He outlined a personal loan option with a reasonable interest rate and a flexible repayment plan. Aarya nodded along, only half-listening. He wasn't worried about the terms of the loan. All he could think about was the money, the fresh capital he would soon have at his disposal. It was the key to getting back on track.

By the end of the week, the money was in his account.

The rush of excitement he felt was familiar, similar to the high he'd experienced after his first successful trade. For the first time in weeks, he felt like he had some control over his situation again. He had the capital, the knowledge, and the determination. All he needed was a little luck and a few well-timed trades.

Aarya spent the next few days glued to his computer, scanning the market for opportunities. He read articles, scoured forums, and watched videos from self-proclaimed experts. The tension in his body built as he immersed himself in the world of stock trading once again. Every tick of the market felt like a drumbeat, pushing him toward his next move.

He found himself gravitating toward riskier plays—small-cap stocks that had the potential for explosive growth but came with a higher chance of collapse. He rationalized the risk by telling himself that high risk meant high reward. After all, he wasn't trying to make incremental gains. He needed to make a big move, fast, to justify the loan he had taken out. There was no room for caution. Not anymore.

His first trade with the borrowed money seemed to validate his decision. He invested a sizable portion of his loan into a tech startup that had been generating buzz online. The stock surged within hours of his purchase, and Aarya watched in awe as his portfolio grew by 15% in a single day.

This was it. This was the moment he had been waiting for.

The exhilaration was short-lived. Over the next few days, the stock's momentum slowed, and the price began to drop. Aarya was torn between holding on, hoping for a recovery, or selling to lock in his small profit. Anxiety gnawed at him as he refreshed the page again and again, watching the price fluctuate.

In the end, he sold. The gain was modest, nothing compared to what he had hoped for, but it was still a profit. He convinced himself that this was just the beginning, that he could repeat this success on a larger scale. The borrowed money wasn't a burden yet—it was his ticket to financial freedom.

But with every passing trade, the stakes grew higher. Aarya started making decisions based on fear and desperation rather than careful analysis. He had convinced himself that the loan was an opportunity, but deep down, he knew the truth: it was a ticking time bomb. Every day that passed without a major win increased the pressure. The repayment deadline loomed in the back of his mind, and the knowledge that he was trading with borrowed money weighed heavily on him.

The pressure to perform, to make enough money to cover his debts and still come out ahead, was relentless. He became obsessed with the market, checking his account constantly, even at work. His productivity at his office job declined, but he didn't care. The job felt like a distraction from what really mattered—recovering his losses and proving to himself that he could succeed as a trader.

One evening, after a particularly volatile day in the market, Aarya found himself lying awake in bed, staring at the ceiling. His mind raced with thoughts of all the trades he had made, the mistakes, the missed opportunities. He thought about the loan, the growing interest, and the realization that he was deeper in the hole than ever before.

How had it come to this?

The turning point came a few weeks later. Aarya had been following a pharmaceutical stock that had shown promising signs of growth. There was a buzz around a new drug the company was developing, and the stock price had already begun to rise in anticipation of positive news from the FDA. Aarya saw this as his chance. If the drug was approved, the stock would skyrocket, and he would finally make the kind of gains that would put his debt—and his worries—behind him.

He went all in.

It was the largest trade he had ever made, and the weight of it hung on his shoulders like an anchor. The next few days were agonizing. He couldn't think about anything else, couldn't focus on work, couldn't relax at home. Every time he checked the stock, it felt like his heart was going to leap out of his chest.

Then the news came in: the drug had failed to get FDA approval.

The stock plummeted.

Aarya stared at the screen in disbelief as his portfolio bled red. He had lost nearly everything, and this time, there was no recovery in sight. The reality of his situation hit him like a freight train. Not only had he lost his capital, but he also owed money—money he didn't have—to the bank. The loan that had once felt like a lifeline now hung around his neck like a noose.

As the days passed, Aarya fell into a deep depression. He avoided his friends and family, too ashamed to tell them what had happened. He stopped going to work, taking sick days to stay home and wallow in his failure. The phone calls from the bank began, at first polite reminders of his upcoming payment, then increasingly insistent demands for repayment.

Aarya felt trapped. He had gambled with money he didn't have, chasing the dream of quick wealth, and now he was paying the price. The stock market had lured him in with promises of financial freedom, but it had taken everything from him—his money, his confidence, and his peace of mind.

He had reached the end of the line, and the weight of his debt pressed down on him with unbearable force.

In the weeks that followed, Aarya tried to piece together the fragments of his life. He made arrangements with the bank to restructure his loan, but the payments still felt like an insurmountable burden. He returned to his office job, but the passion he once had for escaping the 9-to-5 grind was gone. He had been humbled, broken by the market that had once seemed like his path to freedom.

Aarya had learned the hard way that trading with borrowed money was like walking on a razor's edge. The margin for error was too thin, and the risks too high. He had overleveraged himself, placing his future in the hands of a volatile, unpredictable market, and it had chewed him up and spit him out.

As he sat at his desk one evening, staring at the spreadsheet that had once symbolized his ambition, Aarya realized that his dream of trading success had turned into a nightmare. He had borrowed time, borrowed money, and borrowed hope.

And now, it was time to pay the price.

Chapter 6: A Flicker of Hope

The weeks following Aarya's disastrous loss felt like an endless tunnel, devoid of light or direction. Each morning, he woke with the same hollow feeling in his chest—the weight of debt, failure, and hopelessness dragging him down. But despite the heaviness that clouded his mind, there was one thought that refused to leave him: the idea that he could still recover. If only he played his cards right, if only he could figure out the market, maybe—just maybe—there was a way to claw his way back.

His days were spent juggling the demands of his job and the relentless pressure of repaying his loans. His nights were consumed by the stock market, scrolling through charts, reading analysis after analysis, searching for patterns that might offer him a way out. It was during one of these long, sleepless nights that Aarya stumbled upon an opportunity.

A stock he had been quietly monitoring for a few weeks was beginning to show signs of life. It was a small-cap company in the tech sector—nothing too flashy, but it had made some moves that piqued his interest. The company had just announced a new product launch, and whispers of potential partnerships were spreading through online forums. Aarya hesitated at first. After everything that had happened, he was wary of making another trade, especially with the little capital he had left.

But then he saw it—the chart pattern he had read about countless times in trading guides. A bullish breakout was forming, the kind that could lead to a sharp increase in the stock price. His pulse quickened. This was the opportunity he had been waiting for. He could feel it. He couldn't afford to miss out on this one.

Taking a deep breath, Aarya placed a small trade. It wasn't much—he couldn't risk what little money he had left—but it was enough to give him a stake in the game. As the hours passed, he watched the stock price inch upward, slowly at first, then gaining momentum. His heart pounded with every tick. The emotions that had been dulled by weeks of despair started to resurface—hope, excitement, and the rush of possibility.

By the end of the day, Aarya's trade had netted him a modest profit.

It wasn't a life-changing amount by any stretch, but in that moment, it felt like a victory. After weeks of losses and crushing defeats, he had finally come out on top. The flicker of hope that had been extinguished by his previous failures began to glow again, faint but persistent.

The following days brought a renewed sense of purpose. Aarya's confidence, though fragile, began to rebuild. He spent hours researching, poring over stock analysis reports, reading up on market trends, and honing his trading strategies. He knew he had to be careful. His earlier mistakes had been the result of overconfidence and impulsive decisions, and he couldn't afford to fall into the same traps again.

But the market had a way of drawing traders back in, and Aarya was no exception. His recent success, however small, had given him a taste of victory, and the hunger for more was growing. His mind buzzed with the possibility that he could recover faster than he had initially thought. If he could string together a series of small wins, he could chip away at his debt and rebuild his portfolio. All he needed was a bit of luck and the right trades.

One evening, after a particularly good day in the market, Aarya decided to increase his position in the same tech stock that had brought him his recent success. The company's product launch had been well-received, and there were rumors of a major acquisition that could send the stock price soaring. His cautious approach from earlier had given way to a new sense of optimism. He convinced himself that the risks were manageable, that the stock was poised for further gains, and that this was his chance to capitalize.

This time, he invested more heavily.

The following morning, Aarya watched as the stock continued its upward trajectory. Every time the price ticked higher, he felt a surge of excitement. The profit was rolling in, and for the first time in what felt like ages, he was seeing real progress. His portfolio was growing, slowly but surely, and his confidence was following suit.

But as the day wore on, the stock's momentum began to stall. The price fluctuated, moving sideways, and Aarya's excitement turned into nervousness. He had been here before, in this exact position—riding the high of a successful trade, only to watch it crumble as the market turned against him. His instincts told him to sell, to lock in the profit he had made before it disappeared. But something held him back.

Aarya had been reading about the concept of "holding your winners," a strategy that advised traders to let their successful trades run rather than selling too soon. He had cut his profits short too many times in the past, and he wasn't going to make the same mistake again. The stock still had potential, he told himself. The rumors of the acquisition were gaining traction, and the price could skyrocket any day now.

So he held on.

The next few days were agonizing. The stock fluctuated wildly, swinging between gains and losses, and Aarya found himself checking the price constantly, unable to focus on anything else. Every dip in the price sent a jolt of anxiety through him, while every rise reignited his hope. It was an emotional roller-coaster, but Aarya couldn't bring himself to sell. He had convinced himself that this was the trade that would turn everything around.

And then, just as quickly as the stock had risen, it began to fall.

The rumors of the acquisition were debunked. The market reacted swiftly, and the stock price plummeted. Aarya watched in horror as his profits evaporated before his eyes, leaving him with a loss that he couldn't afford to take. Panic set in. He had waited too long, hoping for a bigger payout, and now he was paying the price.

For the first time since his initial losses, Aarya felt the familiar sting of failure. The flicker of hope that had sustained him through the past few weeks began to dim once again. He had believed that his fortunes were turning, that he had finally figured out how to navigate the market, but now it felt like he was back at square one.

The loss wasn't as catastrophic as some of the ones he had suffered in the past, but it was enough to shake his fragile confidence. More than the financial blow, it was the emotional toll that weighed on him. The constant cycle of hope and disappointment was exhausting, and Aarya found himself questioning whether he had the resilience to keep going.

Over the next few days, Aarya struggled to regain his footing. He took a break from trading, not because he wanted to, but because he needed to clear his head. He spent hours reflecting on his journey, trying to make sense of the highs and lows he had experienced. The market was unpredictable—he knew that—but what frustrated him the most was how easily his emotions had swayed his decisions.

He had let his small wins lull him into a false sense of security. He had ignored the warning signs, convinced that he could replicate his success if he just held on a little longer. In hindsight, it was obvious where he had gone wrong, but in the moment, it had felt like he was on the verge of something big.

It was a lesson he had learned before, but one that he needed to learn again: the market didn't care about his hopes or dreams. It didn't owe him anything, and every trade was a gamble, no matter how well-researched it seemed.

Despite the setback, Aarya wasn't ready to give up entirely. There was still a part of him that believed in the possibility of success, even if it seemed more elusive than ever. He had tasted victory, however fleeting, and that taste was enough to keep him in the game.

But he knew he had to change his approach.

The flicker of hope that had reignited his trading ambitions hadn't been extinguished yet. It was dim, but it was still there, glowing faintly in the recesses of his mind. Aarya knew that if he was going to continue, he would have to be smarter, more disciplined, and less swayed by the emotional highs and lows that had plagued him so far.

The stock market had taught him many lessons—some painful, some empowering—but perhaps the most important lesson was that hope, though fragile, could be the most dangerous emotion of all.

And as Aarya stared at the charts on his screen, contemplating his next move, he realized that his journey was far from over.

Chapter 7: When the Sky Falls

The hum of Aarya's computer screen was now a familiar background noise, blending into the sounds of his life as naturally as the ticking of a clock. Days had passed in a blur since his last trade, and though the sting of loss still lingered, he had found a fragile sense of purpose again. The markets, always dynamic and unpredictable, still held a strange allure for him—an ever-present temptation that he couldn't shake off, despite everything.

But the winds were shifting. As the days wore on, the markets seemed to be veering off course, not because of individual company performances or industry trends, but because of factors far beyond the realm of normalcy. The news headlines blared with warnings of a global economic slowdown, political unrest in major economies, and trade wars that threatened to derail the fragile balance of the financial world.

Aarya had never paid much attention to macroeconomic factors before. His focus had always been on individual stocks, micro-trends, and short-term movements. He believed that if he could read the signals of a company's performance correctly, he could stay ahead of the game. But now, it was becoming clear that no stock, no matter how solid, was immune to the shifting tides of global events. The entire market was being swept up in a storm—a storm that Aarya was woefully unprepared for.

The first sign of trouble came on a cold Monday morning. Aarya had woken up early, as he often did now, to check the pre-market activity. He had been optimistic the night before, having placed a few trades based on promising technical indicators. But as soon as he opened his trading platform, his heart sank.

The screen was a sea of red. The indices were down, and so were most of the stocks he had invested in. News of a major political crisis overseas had sent shockwaves through the market, and panic selling had ensued across the globe. Even the stocks that had seemed like sure bets the day before were now plummeting, dragged down by the sheer force of market-wide fear.

Aarya stared at the screen, frozen. His mind raced, trying to make sense of what was happening. He hadn't anticipated this. The charts and patterns he had studied didn't account for political upheaval or economic sanctions. His strategies, built on technical analysis and the assumption of market stability, were unraveling in real-time.

Panic began to set in.

In the days that followed, the markets continued to spiral. The political crisis had sparked a chain reaction that was now affecting economies worldwide. Trade agreements were being called into question, supply chains were disrupted, and investors were pulling their money out of risky assets at an alarming rate. It wasn't just one sector or one country—it was everywhere.

Aarya, still clinging to the hope that the market would recover, hesitated to sell his positions. He had already lost a significant amount of capital, and the thought of locking in those losses was too painful to bear. Besides, he told himself, the market always rebounded eventually. He had seen it before—periods of volatility followed by sharp recoveries. If he could just hold on, things would turn around.

But this time, it was different.

The volatility was more extreme than anything Aarya had experienced. Stocks would plummet one day, only to bounce back slightly the next, giving him false hope, before crashing again. The uncertainty was suffocating, and every decision felt like a gamble. Should he sell and cut his losses, or should he wait for a rebound? Each option seemed equally perilous.

Aarya's debt loomed over him like a dark cloud. The loan he had taken out to recover his earlier losses now felt like a ticking time bomb. Every day that the market didn't recover, the interest on his debt grew, tightening the noose around his financial future. He had once believed that he could trade his way out of this mess, but now, as the global crisis deepened, that belief was slipping away.

By the end of the second week, Aarya's portfolio had been decimated. He had lost nearly 60% of his remaining capital, and the rest was hanging by a thread. The stocks he had invested in, once touted as high-growth opportunities, were now at rock bottom, and there was no clear indication of when—or if—they would recover.

The emotional toll was immense. Aarya found himself in a constant state of anxiety, checking the markets obsessively, even though he knew there was little he could do to control the situation. His appetite had disappeared, and he had trouble sleeping. Every time he closed his eyes, he saw the numbers—the losses mounting, the debt growing, the future slipping away.

His relationships began to suffer as well. Friends and family noticed the change in him. He was more withdrawn, more irritable, and less engaged in the world around him. Conversations with his wife, once filled with plans for the future, had become terse and strained. She could see the toll the market was taking on him, but Aarya, consumed by the weight of his financial burden, could hardly bring himself to talk about it.

"What are we going to do, Aarya?" she asked him one night, her voice filled with concern.

"I'm handling it," he replied, though the words felt hollow even as he spoke them.

But the truth was, he wasn't handling it. He was barely holding on.

As the global turmoil continued, Aarya found himself turning to riskier and riskier strategies in a desperate attempt to recover. He began day trading, trying to capitalize on the extreme volatility by buying and selling stocks within minutes, hoping to catch small gains in a market that was swinging wildly in both directions. It was a dangerous game, and one that required precision, discipline, and nerves of steel—qualities that Aarya, in his frazzled state, no longer possessed.

His trades became erratic, driven more by emotion than logic. He would buy into a stock as it spiked, only to watch it crash moments later. He would sell in a panic, only to see the stock rebound shortly after. The market, which had once seemed like a puzzle he could solve, now felt like a chaotic storm, where nothing made sense and every decision led to more loss.

The pressure was mounting from all sides. His broker had issued a margin call, demanding that he either deposit more funds or sell off his remaining positions to cover the losses. But Aarya had no more funds to deposit, and the thought of selling off what little he had left felt like admitting defeat.

The breaking point came on a Friday afternoon.

Aarya had placed a large, leveraged bet on a stock that he believed was poised for a recovery. The company had announced some positive news, and the stock had surged in the pre-market trading. Aarya, seeing an opportunity, had gone all-in, convinced that this was the trade that would save him.

But as the trading day began, the stock's momentum faltered. Aarya watched in disbelief as the price, which had been rising steadily just hours before, began to drop. At first, it was a small dip, nothing to worry about. But then, like a dam breaking, the price plummeted.

In a matter of minutes, the stock had lost nearly half of its value, wiping out Aarya's position and triggering the margin call he had been dreading. His account was now in the red, and there was nothing he could do to stop it.

Aarya stared at the screen, numb. The market had taken everything—his savings, his hopes, his sense of control. The reality of his situation hit him like a tidal wave. He was broke, in debt, and completely powerless.

That evening, as the sun set on yet another disastrous day in the market, Aarya sat in silence, his mind racing. The dream of financial freedom that had once driven him was now a distant memory, replaced by the cold, hard truth of his failure. The sky had fallen, and he was left standing in the wreckage, unsure of how to rebuild.

For the first time in months, Aarya allowed himself to consider the possibility that there was no coming back from this. The debt was too great, the losses too deep. He had gambled everything on a dream, and now that dream had turned into a nightmare.

And yet, somewhere in the back of his mind, a flicker of hope remained. Perhaps it was the same stubborn optimism that had kept him in the market for so long, or perhaps it was the simple refusal to accept defeat. But even in the face of overwhelming odds, Aarya couldn't bring himself to give up completely.

The market had broken him, but it hadn't destroyed him. Not yet.

And as the night wore on, Aarya began to realize that his journey was far from over. The road ahead would be difficult, and the odds were stacked against him. But if there was one thing he had learned, it was that the market was unpredictable—and that meant there was always a chance, however slim, that the tide could turn once again.

For better or worse, Aarya was still in the game.

Chapter 8: The Abyss

Aarya sat motionless at his desk, the soft hum of his computer fading into the background as his mind wandered through a labyrinth of despair. The screen before him, once alive with possibilities and excitement, now seemed a cold and unforgiving reminder of the many mistakes he had made. The charts, the news feeds, the blinking numbers—all of it had become a blur, symbols of a world that had chewed him up and spit him out.

He had lost everything. The hopes and dreams that once fueled his passion for trading had been decimated by a series of catastrophic losses, leaving him buried under a mountain of debt. He had started this journey with visions of financial freedom and independence, but now, sitting alone in the dim light of his small apartment, all he could feel was the weight of his failure.

Aarya's debts had reached a point where even his minimal expenses had become a burden. The loan payments, the interest, the margin calls—it all piled up like an insurmountable wall, trapping him in a reality that felt suffocating. The thought of quitting, of leaving the market behind for good, had crossed his mind more times than he cared to admit. Maybe it was time to accept that he wasn't cut out for this, that he had made a terrible mistake chasing a dream that was never really his to achieve.

But even in the darkest recesses of his mind, Aarya struggled with the idea of quitting. There was something about the market—its complexity, its unpredictability—that still pulled at him. It was like a puzzle he couldn't solve, but one that he was desperate to figure out. His failures, painful as they were, hadn't killed his curiosity. If anything, they had only deepened his desire to understand what he had done wrong.

Yet, curiosity alone wasn't enough to climb out of the abyss he had fallen into. The weight of his losses, both financial and emotional, pressed down on him like a boulder, crushing any hope he had left. His confidence, once brimming, had been shattered. Now, every decision felt like a potential catastrophe, every trade a gamble that could push him further into debt.

It was on one of these soul-crushing days that Aarya found himself wandering the streets of the city, seeking a distraction from the endless spiral of self-doubt and regret that occupied his mind. The bustling crowd moved around him in a blur, each person engrossed in their own life, oblivious to the turmoil brewing inside him. He felt disconnected from it all, like a ghost drifting through the world with no real place in it.

As he wandered aimlessly, he passed a small café tucked away in a quiet corner of the city. It was an unassuming place, with wooden tables and large windows that let in the afternoon sun. Something about the peaceful atmosphere drew Aarya in, and without thinking, he stepped inside.

The café was nearly empty, save for a few patrons scattered about, quietly sipping their drinks and reading the day's news. Aarya found a seat near the window, ordered a coffee, and sat down, lost in his thoughts.

He had been sitting there for what felt like hours when an older man approached his table. The man looked to be in his late fifties or early sixties, with graying hair and a calm, steady presence. He carried an air of quiet authority, the kind that came from years of experience and a deep understanding of the world.

"Mind if I sit here?" the man asked, gesturing to the empty chair across from Aarya.

Aarya nodded, surprised by the request but too drained to care. The man sat down and, after a moment of silence, spoke again.

"You've got the look of someone who's been through the wringer," he said, his tone light but not unkind.

Aarya glanced up, meeting the man's eyes for the first time. There was something in the older man's gaze—a mixture of empathy and understanding—that caught him off guard.

"I suppose you could say that," Aarya replied, his voice low. "Just... trying to figure things out."

The man smiled, a small, knowing smile. "The market has a way of doing that to people. It breaks you down, makes you question everything you thought you knew."

Aarya's heart skipped a beat. How did this man know about his struggles with the market? He hadn't said anything about trading, yet it was as if the man could see right through him.

"I've been there," the man continued. "I've seen what the market can do to someone who's unprepared, who goes in thinking it's all about quick wins and easy money."

Aarya's curiosity piqued. "You trade?"

"I used to," the man said, leaning back in his chair. "For over thirty years. I've seen it all—the booms, the crashes, the panic and the euphoria. Made plenty of mistakes along the way, just like everyone else."

For the first time in weeks, Aarya felt a spark of hope. This man—whoever he was—seemed to understand what he was going through. Maybe, just maybe, he could offer some guidance.

"What happened?" Aarya asked, leaning forward slightly. "How did you get through it?"

The man paused, as if considering how much to reveal. Then, with a deep breath, he began to speak.

"I'll tell you a story," the man said, his voice calm and steady. "There was a time, early in my trading career, when I thought I had it all figured out. I was young, full of confidence, and making money hand over fist. I thought I was invincible."

He paused, taking a sip of his coffee before continuing. "But then, the market turned. I lost everything in a matter of weeks. All my profits, gone. My savings, wiped out. I was devastated. For the first time in my life, I felt completely lost. I thought about quitting—hell, I was ready to walk away and never look back."

Aarya listened intently, the man's words echoing his own experiences. He had felt the same way, that crushing sense of defeat, the urge to give up and abandon the dream that had once seemed so within reach.

"But then," the man continued, "I met someone—a veteran trader, much like myself now. He saw the potential in me, even when I couldn't see it in myself. He took me under his wing and taught me things I hadn't learned in all the books and seminars. He taught me patience. Discipline. The importance of strategy over instinct."

The man's eyes softened as he spoke, as if remembering the lessons he had learned from his own mentor. "That's the thing about trading. It's not just about the numbers, the charts, or the technical analysis. It's about your mindset. How you handle the losses, the uncertainty, the fear. It's about knowing when to act and when to wait."

Aarya felt a strange sense of relief wash over him. For so long, he had been fighting the market, trying to outsmart it, control it. But maybe that was the wrong approach. Maybe, instead of fighting, he needed to learn how to navigate it with more care, more wisdom.

"Look," the man said, his voice gentle but firm. "I'm not saying it's easy. It's not. The market will test you, push you to your limits. But if you learn to approach it with the right mindset, if you're willing to be patient and disciplined, you can succeed. You just need to stop chasing the quick wins and start focusing on the long game."

Aarya nodded slowly, absorbing the man's words. The truth of them resonated deep within him, striking a chord that had long been out of tune.

"I don't know if I can do it," Aarya admitted, his voice barely above a whisper. "I've made so many mistakes. I'm in so much debt. I don't even know where to start."

The man leaned forward, his gaze steady. "You start by letting go of the past. The mistakes you've made, the money you've lost—that's all behind you now. What matters is what you do next. You've got potential, I can see it. But you need to stop letting your emotions drive your decisions. You need a plan, a strategy."

Aarya felt a flicker of hope, a tiny spark that had been buried under layers of doubt and fear. Could it really be that simple? Could a change in mindset, a shift in strategy, turn things around?

"How do I begin?" Aarya asked, his voice tinged with both hope and hesitation.

The man smiled again, a kind, reassuring smile. "You start by learning. Not from forums or self-proclaimed experts, but from those who've been in the trenches, those who've made the mistakes and survived to tell the tale. You need to rebuild your foundation, brick by brick. And I'll help you—if you're willing to listen."

Aarya's heart raced. For the first time in what felt like an eternity, he felt a glimmer of something he had thought was lost: hope. The road ahead would be long, and the debt wouldn't disappear overnight, but maybe—just maybe—he could find a way to climb out of the abyss.

In the weeks that followed, Aarya met with the man—whom he learned was named Raj—on a regular basis. Each meeting was a lesson in patience, discipline, and humility. Raj taught him how to approach the market with a clear mind, free from the noise of fear and greed. He introduced Aarya to the concept of risk management, showing him how to protect his capital and avoid the devastating losses that had plagued his earlier trades.

Slowly but surely, Aarya began to rebuild. His trades became more calculated, more thoughtful. He no longer chased after quick wins, but focused on long-term growth, accepting that losses were part of the process, not the end of the road.

It wasn't easy. There were days when the market still seemed like an insurmountable force, when the weight of his debts and the memory of his failures threatened to pull him back into the abyss. But with Raj's guidance, Aarya learned to navigate those dark moments, to trust in the process and keep moving forward.

And though he was still far from where he wanted to be, for the first time in a long while, Aarya felt like he was on the right path. The abyss was no longer his home—it was a place he had visited, learned from, and left behind.

Chapter 9: The Long Game

The lessons from Raj marked the beginning of a new chapter in Aarya's trading journey, not just in practice but in mindset. As the days turned into weeks and the weeks into months, Aarya found himself trading less frequently but with far more precision and care. His once haphazard approach—filled with impulsive decisions and reactive behavior—had been replaced by a calm, measured strategy. He was no longer chasing the adrenaline rush of quick profits but was focused on something far more valuable: sustainability.

Sitting at his desk, Aarya's environment looked the same—the same screens, the same charts, the same patterns of market movement—but his internal world had shifted dramatically. He now looked at the blinking numbers on his screen with the detachment of a seasoned observer, not as a gambler anxiously awaiting his next big score.

The Shift in Mindset

The first change Raj had instilled in Aarya was patience. In their conversations, Raj often emphasized that successful traders weren't the ones who made the most trades, but the ones who made the right trades. It was a subtle but powerful distinction. Aarya had once believed that activity equated to progress—he felt the more trades he placed, the closer he would get to his goals. But Raj had quickly dispelled that myth.

"You don't need to be in the market every day," Raj had told him during one of their early sessions. "Sometimes, the best trade you can make is no trade at all."

Aarya was initially puzzled by this philosophy, but as he practiced it, the truth of Raj's words became evident. He had learned to wait for the right setups, the right conditions, and the right opportunities, rather than forcing trades out of a need to 'stay in the game.' This shift alone had significantly reduced his losses. He no longer fell victim to emotional impulses or panic-induced decisions.

The second lesson was discipline, particularly when it came to risk management. Raj's approach to risk was almost religious in its rigor. He had a golden rule that Aarya had quickly adopted: never risk more than 1% of your capital on any single trade. At first, Aarya found this overly conservative, but Raj had explained it with the kind of clarity that only comes from decades of experience.

"In the market, survival is the name of the game," Raj had said. "If you protect your capital, you live to trade another day. But if you're reckless, if you treat every trade like a gamble, you'll be wiped out before you even have a chance to learn."

The importance of preserving capital became one of Aarya's core principles. He realized that the market wasn't something to be conquered—it was something to be respected. By setting strict stop losses and sticking to his risk limits, Aarya was no longer in constant danger of losing everything. His focus had shifted from how much he could win to how little he could afford to lose.

Another major change in Aarya's approach was diversification. Before meeting Raj, Aarya had been laser-focused on a few stocks and sectors, convinced that the more concentrated his portfolio, the higher his potential returns. It was a common mistake among novice traders—a belief that putting all your money in one or two high-risk, high-reward trades was the path to riches.

But Raj had taught him otherwise.

"You can't predict the future," Raj had said, with the calm authority of someone who had weathered more market storms than Aarya could imagine. "No one can. The only way to survive the unpredictability of the market is to spread your risk. Diversification isn't just about making more money—it's about protecting yourself from the unknown."

Aarya had taken this lesson to heart. He began to spread his investments across different asset classes—stocks, bonds,

commodities, and even a small portion in cryptocurrencies. He also diversified geographically, investing in international markets to avoid being overly reliant on any one economy or political system. This strategy reduced his portfolio's volatility, and while it also meant that his returns weren't as explosive as they had been during his earlier, riskier days, they were far more consistent.

It was a strange feeling for Aarya. In the past, he had craved those big, immediate wins that had once seemed so tantalizing but always proved fleeting. Now, he found satisfaction in the slow, steady growth of his portfolio. It wasn't the kind of success that came with fireworks or instant gratification, but it was real, tangible progress. Each day that passed without a major loss felt like a small victory in itself.

Emotional discipline had been perhaps the hardest lesson for Aarya to learn. In the past, his trading had been dominated by emotions—greed when the market was rising, fear when it was falling, and desperation when things went wrong. He had often found himself caught in the emotional whirlwinds of market sentiment, following the herd mentality, buying when everyone else was buying, and selling in a panic when prices dropped.

Raj, however, had taught him a new way to approach the market—one that was detached from the emotional ups and downs. "The market doesn't care about your feelings," Raj had told him. "It doesn't care if you're scared or excited or desperate. It moves according to its own logic, and the sooner you accept that, the better off you'll be."

Raj had introduced Aarya to the concept of trading plans—predefined strategies that outlined exactly when and why to enter or exit a trade. These plans removed the emotional element from the decision-making process. No longer did Aarya make impulsive decisions based on fear or greed. Instead, he followed his plan with mechanical precision. If a trade hit his stop loss, he exited without hesitation. If a trade reached his target, he took profits without second-guessing himself.

The hardest part was learning to accept small losses. There were days when Aarya's trades didn't go as planned, when the market moved against him in ways he hadn't anticipated. In the past, he would have panicked, desperately trying to 'make back' his losses by placing more risky trades. But now, with Raj's guidance, he understood that small losses were just part of the game. The key was to keep them small and not let them spiral out of control.

Each loss, no matter how frustrating, was a learning opportunity. With each mistake, Aarya became a little wiser, a little more disciplined. Over time, he developed a thick skin, able to weather the inevitable downturns without losing his composure. The emotional roller-coaster that had once defined his trading life was now a thing of the past.

Months passed, and Aarya's portfolio, though still modest, began to show signs of life. His capital was no longer hemorrhaging, and though his profits were slow and steady, they were far more consistent than the wild swings he had experienced in the past. He had built a solid foundation, and for the first time in a long while, he felt a sense of control over his financial future.

Aarya's daily routine reflected this newfound approach. Each morning, he would spend hours analyzing the markets, not in a frantic rush to find the next big trade but with a calm, methodical eye. He would review his charts, follow the news, and assess his positions. He took the time to research the companies he was investing in, understanding their fundamentals rather than relying solely on technical indicators or market hype.

This slow, deliberate approach was a far cry from the frantic, reactive style of trading he had once employed. And it was paying off. His portfolio wasn't growing at an exponential rate, but it was growing steadily—and that was enough. The consistency was more satisfying than any single big win could have been.

Raj had been right all along. The market wasn't about getting rich quickly—it was about surviving, learning, and playing the long game. Aarya's goal had shifted from making as much money as possible in the shortest amount of time to building a sustainable financial future, one that could weather the inevitable storms and uncertainties of the market.

One of the most significant changes in Aarya's approach was his commitment to always having a plan. Before every trade, he outlined his entry point, his stop loss, his target price, and his reasons for making the trade. This forced him to think critically about each decision, removing the emotional impulsiveness that had once led to so many disastrous trades.

Having a plan also helped Aarya stay disciplined during market downturns. When the market moved against him, he didn't panic or scramble to make up for losses with reckless trades. Instead, he trusted his plan and stuck to his risk management rules. This not only protected his capital but also gave him a sense of control and confidence that had been sorely lacking in his earlier trading days.

Raj had often reminded him that the market was unpredictable and that no strategy could guarantee success 100% of the time. But a good plan, combined with solid risk management, could tip the odds in your favor over the long term.

"The market isn't about being right all the time," Raj had said. "It's about being right enough of the time and managing your risks so that when you're wrong, it doesn't wipe you out."

As Aarya continued to implement the lessons he had learned, his trading began to feel less like a gamble and more like a craft—something that could be mastered with time, patience, and practice. He wasn't looking for shortcuts anymore. The thrill of chasing quick profits had been replaced by the quiet satisfaction of seeing his portfolio grow slowly but steadily.

The long game wasn't easy, and it required a level of discipline that Aarya had once thought impossible for himself. But it was worth it. The emotional highs and lows that had once defined his trading life had been replaced by a sense of calm and control. And for the first time, Aarya felt like he was truly on the path to success—not just in trading, but in life.

The journey was far from over, but Aarya now understood that the road to success wasn't a straight line. It was a long, winding path, filled with obstacles and setbacks. But with the right mindset, the right strategy, and the right guidance, it was a path he could navigate. He was in it for the long game now—and that made all the difference.

Chapter 10: The Phoenix Rises

Aarya sat at his desk, staring at the familiar screen of market charts and data points. There was a calm in his demeanor, a quiet sense of purpose that hadn't been there during his earlier trading days. It was a strange feeling, trading without the urgency, without the frenetic energy that had once dominated his decision-making process. The frantic highs and devastating lows had been replaced by a steady rhythm, one that mirrored the market's natural ebb and flow.

He had just closed out a trade—not a large one, but it was profitable. The satisfaction that came with the green numbers on his screen wasn't the explosive thrill he used to feel, but something much more grounded: the quiet confidence of someone who knew they were on the right path.

It had been months since Raj had taken Aarya under his wing, teaching him the principles of patience, discipline, and strategic thinking. Slowly but surely, Aarya had begun to rebuild his capital, one small trade at a time. The heady days of chasing quick profits were behind him. He now understood that the road to financial recovery wasn't about dramatic comebacks or high-risk gambles. It was about steady, consistent progress.

His first few profitable trades after his major losses had felt almost surreal. They weren't particularly large wins—maybe a few hundred dollars at a time—but they represented something far more important: proof that his new approach worked. Each small victory was a step toward rebuilding his confidence, and, more importantly, a step away from the reckless habits that had once defined his trading.

Raj had warned him that the process of recovery would be slow, but that was exactly the point. The quick wins were often the most dangerous, luring traders into a false sense of security and encouraging risky behavior. The long game was about building a foundation that could withstand the inevitable storms that the market would throw at him.

Aarya had learned to appreciate the slow accumulation of profits. He no longer measured his success in terms of single trades or daily gains. Instead, he evaluated his progress over weeks and months, focusing on the bigger picture. His profits were smaller than they had been during his earlier, more reckless days, but they were consistent—and consistency, he had learned, was the true mark of success in the market.

As his trading portfolio began to grow, Aarya turned his attention to the mountain of debt that had accumulated during his darkest days. It was a constant weight on his shoulders, a reminder of the mistakes he had made and the consequences that followed. But rather than feeling overwhelmed, Aarya approached the task of paying off his debts with the same discipline and strategy he had applied to his trading.

The first step was to prioritize. Some debts were more urgent than others—those with high interest rates or those that could damage his credit if left unpaid. He created a detailed plan, allocating a portion of his trading profits toward each debt in a methodical way. It wasn't glamorous, and it certainly wasn't easy, but with each payment, he felt a little lighter, a little freer.

In the past, Aarya had viewed his debts with a sense of panic. They had seemed insurmountable, a crushing burden that he couldn't escape. But now, with his newfound discipline, he saw them as just another challenge—one that could be overcome with patience and persistence. Each payment was a victory, a sign that he was moving in the right direction.

As the months passed, the balances on his debts began to shrink. The process was slow, but it was steady. Aarya no longer felt the overwhelming anxiety that had once plagued him. He knew that he was making progress, and that was enough to keep him motivated.

One of the most profound changes in Aarya's mindset was his newfound confidence in discipline. In the past, he had equated confidence with boldness, with the willingness to take risks and go all-in on a trade. But Raj had taught him that true confidence came from knowing your limits, from sticking to your plan even when the market tempted you to stray.

Aarya had learned to trust his system. He no longer felt the need to chase every opportunity or react to every market movement. He had developed a set of rules that guided his trading decisions, and he followed those rules with unwavering discipline. There were times when the market seemed to offer tantalizing opportunities—highly volatile stocks or sudden price swings—but Aarya no longer gave in to the temptation.

"Discipline is what separates the professionals from the amateurs," Raj had told him. "Anyone can get lucky once or twice, but if you want to make it in this game for the long haul, you need to be consistent. And consistency comes from discipline."

Aarya had taken those words to heart. He no longer saw discipline as a limitation but as a source of freedom. By sticking to his plan, he had freed himself from the emotional roller-coaster that had once controlled his trading. He didn't need to rely on luck or hope for the market to move in his favor. His strategy, based on careful analysis and risk management, provided him with a sense of security that he had never experienced before.

Aarya's financial recovery was only one part of his journey. The fallout from his earlier failures had affected not just his bank account but his relationships as well. His friends and family had watched as he spiraled into debt, consumed by his obsession with trading. He had withdrawn from them, embarrassed by his failures and too proud to ask for help.

But as he began to rebuild his life, Aarya realized that his relationships were just as important as his financial recovery. He reached out to his family, apologizing for the distance he had created and acknowledging the mistakes he had made. It wasn't an easy conversation, but it was a necessary one.

His parents, who had been quietly supportive even during his lowest points, were relieved to see him taking responsibility for his actions. They didn't care about the money—what mattered to them was that Aarya was finding his way back to himself. His friends, too, welcomed him back into their lives, understanding that everyone goes through difficult times and that Aarya's journey had been a learning experience.

Rebuilding these relationships wasn't an overnight process. Just as with his trading and debt repayment, it required patience and effort. But Aarya approached it with the same mindset: one step at a time, with a focus on long-term growth rather than quick fixes.

One of the most important lessons Aarya had learned during his journey was the importance of self-care. In the past, he had thrown himself into trading with reckless abandon, neglecting his health, his sleep, and his mental well-being. The market had consumed him, leaving little room for anything else.

But Raj had emphasized the importance of balance. "You can't trade well if you're not taking care of yourself," he had said. "Your mind is your most important asset, and if you're running on empty, you'll make mistakes."

Aarya had started to incorporate healthier habits into his daily routine. He made time for exercise, knowing that physical health was closely tied to mental clarity. He started meditating, a practice that helped him stay calm and focused even during the most volatile market conditions. He also made sure to take breaks from trading, allowing himself time to recharge and gain perspective.

These changes had a profound impact on his trading performance. He found that he was able to think more clearly, make better decisions, and stay calm under pressure. The market no longer dictated his emotions; he was in control, both of his trading and his life.

As Aarya's capital continued to grow, he found himself in a position he hadn't imagined just a year earlier: one of stability. He wasn't rich, and he wasn't making the kind of money that had once seemed so tantalizing during his reckless days, but he was secure. His portfolio was growing steadily, and his debts were shrinking. He was no longer worried about losing everything in a single bad trade.

This newfound stability gave Aarya a sense of peace. He no longer felt the need to prove anything to himself or to others. He was content with his progress, knowing that real success wasn't about how fast you could rise but how long you could stay in the game.

He had learned to appreciate the slow climb. Each day brought new challenges, but Aarya approached them with the calm confidence of someone who had been through the worst and come out stronger on the other side. He knew that there would be setbacks—there always were in the market—but he also knew that he was prepared for them.

Aarya's journey was far from over. The market was a constantly evolving landscape, and there was always more to learn, more to improve. But for the first time, Aarya felt like he was truly in control of his future. He had risen from the ashes of his earlier failures, and while his path wasn't always easy, it was one that he had forged through discipline, patience, and perseverance.

The phoenix had risen, not in a blaze of glory, but in the steady, deliberate way of someone who understood that real success was built over time, not overnight. And as Aarya looked toward the future, he knew that he was ready for whatever came next.

Chapter 11: Temptation's Lure

Aarya sat in his trading room, the glow of his multiple monitors casting a soft light in the otherwise dim room. The market charts flickered with their endless dance of green and red, each movement signaling opportunity or risk. The steady hum of his routine had settled into a rhythm he had come to rely on, his trades slow, calculated, and deliberate.

But today, there was something different—a flicker on the horizon that caught his attention. A particular stock had made headlines, sending ripples through the market with the promise of explosive returns. The financial news networks buzzed with excitement about an upcoming acquisition in the tech sector. The speculation was rampant, and everyone seemed to agree: this stock was going to skyrocket.

Aarya felt the familiar pang of temptation grip him. The stock had risen rapidly over the past few days, and if the rumors were true, it could go even higher. His disciplined approach—focusing on long-term, slow gains—felt inadequate in the face of this potential windfall. He could already see the numbers multiplying in his head. If he took a sizable position now and rode the wave, he could make more in one trade than he had in months of careful, methodical trading.

The thought excited him, but it also scared him. He knew this feeling all too well. It was the same rush that had driven him into reckless trading before, the same thrill that had cost him nearly everything. Yet, here it was again, tempting him, whispering in his ear that maybe this time, things would be different.

Aarya sat back in his chair, letting out a slow breath. He knew he was at a crossroads. His recent success had been hard-earned, built on the foundations of discipline, patience, and a steady approach. He had learned from his mistakes, had rebuilt his capital, and was finally in a place of stability. But the allure of quick, massive profits was pulling at him, challenging everything he had worked to achieve.

His mind raced, torn between two voices. One voice—the disciplined trader he had become—urged caution. It reminded him of the lessons Raj had instilled in him: risk management, strategic thinking, and the long game. This voice was calm, rational, and steady. It told him that there would always be more opportunities and that there was no need to rush.

The other voice—the voice of his past self—was louder, more insistent. It whispered that he couldn't afford to miss out on this opportunity. Everyone was talking about the stock, and the potential for massive gains was real. The market was volatile, yes, but volatility was where fortunes were made. Why sit on the sidelines when he could seize the moment and make a killing?

Aarya clenched his fists, his heart beating faster. He could feel the pull of temptation tightening around him. The rational part of him knew that this was dangerous, that chasing after big wins had always led to disaster in the past. But another part of him—the part that craved excitement, that wanted to prove to himself that he could make it big—was finding it harder and harder to resist.

As he wrestled with his thoughts, Aarya found himself drifting back to the early days of his trading career. He remembered the rush of those first few big wins, the intoxicating feeling of beating the market and seeing his account balance soar. But he also remembered the devastating losses that had followed, the sleepless nights, and the crushing weight of failure when everything fell apart.

It wasn't just the financial loss that had hurt him; it was the emotional toll. The highs had been exhilarating, but the lows had been soul-crushing. He had lost not just money, but also his sense of self-worth. It had taken him months—years, even—to recover from the damage, both to his finances and to his mental health.

Now, sitting at this critical juncture, Aarya realized that the lure of quick profits was the same trap he had fallen into before. The difference was that he now had the wisdom and experience to recognize it for what it was: a siren's call that led to ruin.

But knowing this didn't make the temptation any easier to resist.

The stock continued to climb throughout the day, and with each tick upwards, Aarya felt the pressure mounting. News of the potential acquisition spread like wildfire, and every financial pundit seemed to have an opinion on how high the stock could go. Some predicted a 50% jump; others were more conservative, but still optimistic about double-digit gains in the near term.

Aarya's phone buzzed with messages from other traders in his network. Most of them were talking about the stock, sharing their excitement, their predictions. A few had already jumped in, bragging about how much they were making as the stock surged.

He knew that once he saw others profiting, the temptation would become nearly unbearable. FOMO—the fear of missing out—was a powerful force in trading, and it was beginning to gnaw at him. He didn't want to be the one left behind while others reaped the rewards.

For a moment, he allowed himself to imagine what it would be like if he gave in. If he put a large chunk of his capital into this stock, and it soared as predicted, he could pay off the remainder of his debts in one fell swoop. He could finally have the financial cushion he had been working so hard to build, but so much faster than his current pace.

But that was the problem, wasn't it? The idea that he could take a shortcut, that he could bypass the hard work and discipline that had gotten him this far. It was the same flawed thinking that had nearly destroyed him before.

In the midst of his inner turmoil, Aarya found himself instinctively reaching for his phone to call Raj. His mentor had always been a voice of reason, the steady hand that had guided him through his darkest moments. Raj had taught him the value of patience and long-term thinking, and Aarya knew that if anyone could help him navigate this temptation, it was Raj.

The phone rang twice before Raj answered, his calm, steady voice on the other end instantly soothing Aarya's frayed nerves.

"What's on your mind, Aarya?" Raj asked.

Aarya hesitated for a moment before blurting out, "There's this stock... it's moving fast. Everyone's talking about it. There's a big opportunity here, and I'm struggling. I know I shouldn't, but it's hard to ignore."

Raj was silent for a moment, letting Aarya's words hang in the air. Then he spoke, his voice measured and thoughtful. "Ah, temptation. It never truly goes away, does it?"

Aarya sighed. "No, it doesn't. I thought I had moved past this, but now... it's all I can think about."

Raj chuckled softly. "You're human, Aarya. Temptation is part of the game. Even the most disciplined traders feel it. The difference is in how you respond to it."

"But what if this is a real opportunity? What if I'm missing out on something big?" Aarya asked, the frustration clear in his voice.

Raj's tone remained calm. "Let me ask you this: is this trade part of your strategy? Does it align with the risk management principles we've discussed? Or is this your ego talking, telling you that you need to hit a home run?"

Aarya didn't answer right away. He knew what Raj was getting at. This trade wasn't part of his plan. It wasn't based on careful analysis or risk management. It was driven by greed, by the desire to make a quick fortune without putting in the work.

Raj continued, "The market is full of opportunities, Aarya. But not every opportunity is meant for you. If this trade doesn't fit within your strategy, then it's not your trade. It's as simple as that."

Aarya felt a wave of clarity wash over him. Raj was right. The market would always offer tempting opportunities, but that didn't mean he had to chase them all. He had spent months building a disciplined approach, and this was just another test of that discipline.

Aarya thanked Raj for his advice and hung up the phone. He sat in silence for a few moments, reflecting on the conversation. He knew what he had to do, but that didn't make it any easier.

He opened his trading platform and pulled up the stock that had been the source of his temptation. The price had continued to climb, and for a brief moment, Aarya's resolve wavered. But then he reminded himself of the lessons he had learned. This wasn't about one trade. It was about the long game, about building sustainable success over time.

With a deep breath, Aarya closed the window. He wasn't going to chase this stock. It wasn't part of his strategy, and no matter how tempting it was, he knew that giving in would only lead him back down a dangerous path.

The moment he made the decision, he felt a sense of relief. The internal battle had been exhausting, but he had come out on the other side with his discipline intact. He had resisted the lure of temptation, and in doing so, he had proven to himself that he was truly in control of his trading.

In the days that followed, Aarya watched as the stock continued to rise. There were moments when he questioned his decision, wondering if he had made the wrong call. But he quickly pushed those thoughts aside. He knew that his success wasn't measured by one missed opportunity. It was measured by the consistency and discipline he brought to his trading every day.

A week later, the stock's rise came to an abrupt halt. The rumors of the acquisition had been exaggerated, and the stock price tumbled as quickly as it had climbed. Traders who had rushed in were left scrambling, their dreams of quick riches shattered.

Aarya watched the chaos from the sidelines, grateful for the decision he had made. He had avoided the rollercoaster of emotions that came with chasing quick wins, and he had stayed true to his strategy. In the end, that was what mattered most.

As he closed out another successful, disciplined trade, Aarya smiled to himself. The lure of temptation would always be there, but he had learned how to resist it. And in doing so, he had taken another step toward becoming the trader—and the person—he aspired to be.

Chapter 12: The Fall of Giants

The market opened on a Monday morning, and Aarya could feel a shift in the air. It wasn't something he could pinpoint on any particular chart or economic indicator, but after years of experience, he had developed a sixth sense for these moments. The financial world was on edge, whispers of market instability growing louder, and the usually confident chatter of traders had taken on a more cautious tone.

Aarya sat in his home office, watching the market unfold in real-time. He had learned over the past few years that markets go through cycles of booms and busts, and it was clear that the current one was entering a phase of high volatility. Unlike the last time he had encountered such turbulence, however, he was prepared. He had a strategy, a plan, and more importantly, the emotional discipline to stay the course.

What struck him most in these early days of the storm was not his own performance, but how some of the most seasoned traders—the ones he had once idolized and aspired to emulate—were beginning to struggle. These were people with decades of experience, who had made fortunes in the market, and yet, as the market grew more unstable, they were showing cracks in their armor.

The warning signs began subtly. Some of the market's biggest names, traders who managed billions of dollars in assets, started voicing concerns. On social media, forums, and even in private conversations, Aarya heard whispers about some large funds making bad bets. A few traders, who had built their reputations on riding the highs of bullish markets, were now grappling with losses.

One name, in particular, caught Aarya's attention: Nathan Cooper, a trader who was nothing short of a legend. Cooper had built his empire on aggressive, high-risk trades, and during the bull market, he had become an icon in the industry. His fund was one of the largest, his decisions often dictating market trends, and his every move was scrutinized by traders across the globe. Aarya had

studied Cooper's strategies in his early years, marveling at his ability to seize opportunities and turn them into massive gains.

But as the volatility increased, rumors began to surface that Cooper's fund was in trouble. Some said he had overleveraged his positions, others claimed that he had placed massive bets on a sector that was now in freefall. Aarya, with his new, cautious approach, had long stopped following traders like Cooper. While he once admired their boldness, he had learned through his own failures that such an approach was unsustainable in the long run.

As the week progressed, the market became more chaotic. Stocks that had been darlings of the market were now crashing, and entire sectors were in disarray. Aarya, now focused on managing risk, had diversified his portfolio and was sitting on more cash than usual, waiting for the right opportunities to enter. He no longer felt the need to be constantly in the market. His mentor, Raj, had drilled into him the importance of patience, and Aarya was now watching the chaos unfold with a sense of detachment.

One morning, as he scrolled through market news, Aarya saw the headline: *Cooper's Fund in Crisis: Billions at Risk*. It was the kind of headline that sent shockwaves through the financial world. Cooper, the man who had been untouchable for so long, was now on the verge of collapse. His fund had lost billions in just a matter of days, and investors were pulling their money out in a panic.

Aarya couldn't believe what he was seeing. He had known that even the best traders could suffer losses, but the magnitude of Cooper's downfall was staggering. The man who had been a giant in the industry was now scrambling to save his fund. News outlets were reporting that he had taken on too much risk, betting heavily on a sector that had crumbled under the weight of the market's volatility. His high-leverage trades, which had made him a fortune during the bull market, were now his undoing.

Aarya sat back in his chair, a mixture of disbelief and quiet understanding washing over him. This was the reality of the market. No one, no matter how successful, was immune to failure. The market was an unforgiving force, and those who failed to adapt were destined to fall. He had seen it happen to himself, and now he was witnessing it on a much larger scale.

In the days that followed, the fallout from Cooper's collapse reverberated throughout the financial world. Other traders and funds, many of whom had followed Cooper's aggressive strategies, were also in trouble. Some had been betting on the same sectors, while others had over-leveraged themselves in a similar way. The domino effect was in full swing, and Aarya watched as fund after fund reported massive losses.

What struck Aarya the most, however, was the emotional toll it took on the traders. He followed the social media feeds of several prominent traders, many of whom had been publicly confident and bullish in the months leading up to the collapse. Now, their posts were filled with panic, frustration, and even despair. Some admitted to losing their entire portfolios. Others talked about sleepless nights and the toll it was taking on their mental health.

Aarya could relate. He had been there before, staring at the screen in disbelief as his hard-earned money evaporated before his eyes. He had felt the weight of failure, the crushing realization that he had made the wrong decisions. But he had also learned from those moments, and it was that hard-earned wisdom that was now keeping him afloat.

While the market continued to plunge, Aarya stayed the course. His portfolio, though not immune to the volatility, was holding steady. He had diversified his assets, maintained a healthy cash reserve, and avoided the temptation to chase high-risk trades. His mentor's lessons echoed in his mind: "Survival first, profits second."

He found himself watching in real-time as some of the traders he had once admired faltered. They had become too accustomed to winning, too reliant on the strategies that had worked in the past. When the market turned against them, they were unable to adapt, and the consequences were devastating.

Aarya's journey had brought him to a place where he could now observe the market with a sense of clarity. He had made mistakes, suffered losses, and nearly lost everything, but he had come out the other side stronger and wiser. Watching the fall of market giants like Cooper served as a reminder that no trader, no matter how experienced or successful, was immune to the inherent unpredictability of the market.

But there was another lesson as well—one that Raj had tried to instill in him from the beginning: ego is the enemy. Many of the traders who were now falling had built their success on confidence, sometimes bordering on arrogance. They had made fortunes, and their success had reinforced the belief that they were invincible. But the market had no regard for ego. It was a force of nature, and those who thought they could control it were always the ones who fell hardest.

Aarya realized that his greatest growth as a trader had come not from his successes, but from his failures. It was the losses, the mistakes, and the painful lessons that had shaped him into the trader he was now. He had learned to respect the market, to approach it with humility, and to understand that no one could predict it with certainty.

Watching the collapse of traders like Cooper, Aarya felt a sense of validation. He had resisted the temptation to follow in their footsteps, to chase the big wins and the high-risk strategies.

Instead, he had chosen the path of patience, discipline, and sustainability. And now, as the market continued its turbulent course, he was surviving while others were falling.

Aarya found himself thinking about Raj more and more during this period. His mentor's words of wisdom had been instrumental in guiding him through the ups and downs of his trading journey. One evening, Aarya decided to reach out to him for a conversation. He wanted to share his thoughts, to discuss the fall of Cooper and the other market giants, and to get Raj's perspective on the situation.

They spoke on the phone for nearly an hour, discussing the current state of the market and the lessons that could be learned from the collapse of even the most successful traders.

Raj's voice was calm, as always, and filled with the quiet confidence of someone who had seen it all before.

"Aarya," Raj said, "what you're seeing now is the natural course of the market. It rewards discipline and punishes arrogance. Those traders who built their empires on aggressive strategies, without considering the risks, are now facing the consequences. But that doesn't mean they were bad traders. It just means they forgot one of the most important rules: the market is always bigger than any individual."

Aarya nodded, even though Raj couldn't see him. "I've been watching it all unfold, and it's been a reminder of how fragile success can be. I used to look up to these traders, but now I realize that they made the same mistakes I once did. They just did it on a larger scale."

Raj chuckled softly. "Exactly. But the important thing is that you've learned from your mistakes. You've built a strategy that prioritizes survival, and that's why you're still standing while others are falling."

Aarya felt a sense of pride in hearing those words. He had come a long way since his early days as a reckless trader, and he knew that Raj's guidance had been a crucial part of his journey.

"Remember this," Raj continued, "the market will always go through cycles. There will be periods of extreme volatility, and there will be times of stability. But your job as a trader is to adapt, to stay humble, and to never let success blind you to the risks. If you can do that, you'll be in this game for the long haul."

Aarya smiled as he hung up the phone. He had survived the storm, and more importantly, he had learned how to weather the next one.

As the market continued its turbulent course, Aarya remained vigilant. He watched as more traders fell, unable to adapt to the new reality of a volatile market. But he stayed the course, sticking to his strategy and resisting the temptation to chase the highs and lows.

In the weeks that followed, the market began to stabilize, and Aarya's portfolio reflected the steady, disciplined growth that had become his hallmark. He had survived one of the most chaotic periods in recent memory, and he had done so not by taking risks, but by staying true to the lessons he had learned.

The fall of giants like Cooper served as a stark reminder that success in the market was never guaranteed. But for Aarya, it was also a validation of his journey—a journey that had taken him from the depths of failure to a place of confidence, discipline, and sustainability.

As he looked to the future, Aarya knew that there would be more challenges ahead. The market would continue to test him, and there would always be temptations to return to his old ways. But he was no longer the trader he once was. He had grown, he had learned, and he was ready for whatever came next.

The fall of giants had shown him that even the most successful traders were vulnerable. But it had also shown him that with the right mindset, strategy, and discipline, he could rise above the chaos and build a future that was not dependent on the whims of the market, but on his own resilience and growth.

Chapter 13: The Calm Within the Storm

The first signs of the impending market correction came as whispers, faint ripples that barely caused a stir in the financial waters. Yet, Aarya had seen enough to know that even the smallest ripples could turn into tidal waves. His screens flickered with data, a blend of numbers and charts that to the untrained eye would seem like a chaotic mess. But Aarya had learned to read between the lines. The market, in all its complexity, was communicating—warning of an approaching storm.

It wasn't the first time Aarya had faced such uncertainty, but this time felt different. Not because of the scale of the correction that was looming, but because of his own evolution as a trader. Gone were the days when he'd been consumed by anxiety, staring at his positions with wide-eyed panic, refreshing his trading platform incessantly as the numbers dipped into the red. He had grown beyond that. Now, he sat before his screens with an eerie sense of calm, his mind focused, his emotions reined in.

The market had been on a prolonged bullish run, and for months, traders had ridden the wave of optimism. Stocks surged, valuations skyrocketed, and speculative frenzy gripped the market as traders scrambled to capture quick gains. Many who had entered the market recently knew nothing but success, and it was precisely this unbridled confidence that signaled danger to Aarya. He had been through enough cycles to know that markets, like nature, followed patterns. What rises too fast inevitably falls just as hard.

Economic reports hinted at inflation creeping higher, central banks were murmuring about interest rate hikes, and corporate earnings, while still strong, began to show signs of fatigue. Yet, despite these warning signs, the majority of traders continued to press forward, confident that the bull market would continue indefinitely. Aarya, however, was not so easily swayed by the market's exuberance.

He began making small adjustments to his portfolio, trimming positions in high-risk assets and increasing his cash holdings. His strategy was clear: preserve capital, minimize risk, and wait for the storm to pass. As the first waves of market volatility began to hit, Aarya was ready, his portfolio positioned to withstand the turbulence.

It started slowly—just a few rough trading sessions where the market seemed to stumble, as if tripping over its own feet. Then, like a sudden gust of wind in a brewing storm, the correction hit with full force. Stocks plummeted, and in the span of days, billions of dollars were wiped off the market. Traders who had been riding the highs of speculative gains were caught off guard, their positions decimated as the market corrected itself.

Aarya watched it all unfold, but instead of fear or panic, he felt a deep sense of focus. He had been here before, in the throes of market chaos, but this time he wasn't the same reckless trader trying to chase every opportunity. He had become a different person—calmer, more calculated, and most importantly, more patient.

In contrast, the broader market was in a state of panic. Social media exploded with posts from traders lamenting their losses. News outlets were flooded with stories of fortunes evaporating overnight, and analysts debated whether this was the beginning of a prolonged downturn. Margin calls were triggered for many traders, forcing them to sell assets at fire-sale prices, further exacerbating the market decline. The air was thick with fear, and in the midst of it all, Aarya remained unmoved.

Aarya's approach during the correction was methodical. He didn't need to make any drastic moves because he had already prepared. Over the past few months, as the market had reached its peak,

Aarya had shifted much of his portfolio into safer, more stable assets. He had reduced exposure to speculative stocks and increased his positions in defensive sectors like utilities and consumer staples—companies that tended to fare better during economic downturns.

As the market correction unfolded, Aarya saw his portfolio drop, but nowhere near the levels of loss that others were experiencing. His risk management strategies were paying off. Instead of panicking and selling off assets, he focused on finding opportunities. With cash reserves on hand, he was in a position to take advantage of the panic-driven sell-off that others were forced into.

During the most volatile days, Aarya would open his trading platform, look at the numbers, and then calmly close his laptop. He had learned the importance of detaching from the emotional swings of the market. It wasn't about chasing every price movement; it was about sticking to a strategy that had been carefully thought out and tested.

Instead of constantly refreshing his trading screens, Aarya spent his time reviewing his long-term investment thesis. He went back to the fundamentals, analyzing the companies in his portfolio, their balance sheets, cash flows, and long-term prospects. He reminded himself that despite the short-term turbulence, the market would eventually recover. It always did. His focus wasn't on surviving this storm but thriving in the aftermath.

As the days passed and the correction deepened, Aarya observed the reactions of other traders. On online forums, where traders had once boasted about their high-flying gains, there was now silence, or worse, admissions of heavy losses. Some of the traders who had been the loudest during the bull run were now facing the harsh reality of margin calls and forced liquidations. These traders, who had once exuded confidence, were now grappling with the consequences of their over-leveraged positions.

Aarya felt a sense of empathy for them. He had been in their shoes before—riding the highs of the market, only to come crashing down when the tide turned. He knew the pain of watching hard-earned money disappear, the sleepless nights spent agonizing over what could have been done differently. But he also knew that it was those painful experiences that had made him a better trader.

One of the most telling moments came when Aarya saw a well-known trader, someone who had been revered in the trading community, announce that they were stepping away from the market indefinitely. This trader had built a reputation on high-risk, high-reward strategies, and while they had enjoyed massive gains during the bull market, they had been utterly crushed by the correction.

For Aarya, this was a stark reminder of the dangers of hubris in the market. No matter how skilled or successful a trader may be, the market is always bigger, always unpredictable. The traders who survive—and thrive—are the ones who respect that unpredictability, who plan for the worst even when the market is at its best.

As the correction continued, word began to spread among Aarya's peers about how well he was handling the situation. He had always been somewhat of an outsider in the trading circles he once tried to break into, but now, traders were reaching out to him for advice. His ability to remain calm, to stick to his plan, and to even make modest gains while others were suffering massive losses had earned him a new level of respect.

In one conversation with a fellow trader, Vikram, who had been hit hard by the correction, Aarya offered words of encouragement. Vikram had been one of the more aggressive traders, constantly chasing the next big opportunity. Now, he was grappling with significant losses and uncertainty about his future in trading.

"Aarya," Vikram said, his voice heavy with frustration, "how are you not panicking? I've seen your portfolio—it's not like you haven't been affected. How do you stay so calm?"

Aarya smiled, not out of arrogance but from a place of understanding. "It's not about avoiding losses entirely, Vikram. Everyone takes hits in a market like this. The key is to manage the losses and not let them overwhelm you. I've been where you are now—chasing every trade, thinking I had to be in the market at all times. But I learned the hard way that the market doesn't care about your plans. It does what it wants."

He paused for a moment, reflecting on his own journey. "What I've learned is that you have to detach from the emotions of trading. Fear, greed, panic—they'll destroy you if you let them. I don't see this correction as a disaster. I see it as an opportunity. You just have to be patient enough to wait for the right moment."

Vikram nodded, though it was clear he was still struggling to process the magnitude of his losses. "I don't know if I have that kind of patience," he admitted.

"It takes time," Aarya said. "But trust me, once you learn to control your emotions, everything changes. The market will always have ups and downs, but if you can keep your cool and stick to your strategy, you'll come out stronger on the other side."

As the market correction began to show signs of stabilizing, Aarya found himself in a strong position. His portfolio had weathered the storm far better than most, and he had even managed to make a small profit by taking advantage of the panic-driven sell-offs. But more than the financial gains, it was the personal growth that mattered most to him.

He had proven to himself that he could stay calm under pressure, that he could navigate through the chaos without falling into the emotional traps that had once led to his downfall. He had become the trader he had always aspired to be—not one who chased every market movement, but one who approached the market with discipline, patience, and a long-term vision.

In the days and weeks that followed, Aarya's reputation continued to grow. Traders who had once dismissed him as a cautious outsider now sought his advice. He had earned their respect not by making bold, reckless trades, but by staying true to his strategy and surviving the storm.

The market would always be unpredictable, always filled with opportunities and dangers. But Aarya had found his calm within the storm, and that calm had become his greatest asset.

Chapter 14: The Ultimate Gamble

The air was thick with anticipation as Aarya sat at his desk, staring at the screen. It had been a long journey to this moment—a journey marked by mistakes, lessons, and a steady evolution into a disciplined trader. The market had thrown countless challenges at him, but he had emerged stronger, more resilient, and more skilled. Yet here he was, on the cusp of a decision that could redefine everything he had worked for.

The news was out: a tech company that had long been a staple in the market was about to announce a groundbreaking product that promised to change the landscape of the industry. Whispers of partnerships with major corporations fueled speculation, and analysts projected that the stock price could double overnight. For Aarya, this was a once-in-a-lifetime opportunity, but it came with a catch—a high-risk gamble that could either lead to unimaginable gains or catastrophic losses.

As he leaned back in his chair, the weight of the decision bore down on him. His mind raced through the implications of this trade. Should he dive in and capitalize on the potential windfall, or should he adhere to the disciplined strategies that had brought him this far? The internal conflict was palpable; the thrill of the gamble beckoned him, yet the voice of reason cautioned against it.

Aarya had always been drawn to the thrill of trading, to the rush of making bold moves and reaping the rewards. But over time, he had learned to temper that thrill with caution, to prioritize discipline and strategic planning over reckless ambition. He had transformed from a trader chasing quick profits into a calculated investor focused on long-term growth.

But now, staring at the news flashing across his screen, he felt the old familiar pull of temptation. This wasn't just any trade; this was a potential game changer. The stock could soar, and with it, his financial dreams could materialize. The gains would not just be

financial; they could validate everything he had learned, everything he had worked for.

Yet, a flicker of doubt crept in. He recalled the lessons from his past mistakes—the reckless decisions driven by emotion, the near ruin that had come from chasing the allure of quick profits. Could he afford to take this risk? Was it worth jeopardizing the progress he had made?

As he contemplated the trade, Aarya dove deep into research. He poured over the company's financials, dissecting balance sheets and income statements. He sought out analysts' reports, trying to discern whether the hype surrounding the product launch was justified. The excitement was palpable; the market sentiment was overwhelmingly positive. But beneath the surface, Aarya found potential red flags—issues with supply chain logistics, doubts about whether the product could meet demand, and a history of over-promising and under-delivering.

Despite these concerns, the potential reward was enormous. If the product truly delivered, the stock could skyrocket, and Aarya's investment could multiply several times over. He felt the tension in his chest as he mulled over the risk-reward ratio. Was he prepared to take a gamble on this opportunity? Could he truly stick to his disciplined strategy in the face of such allure?

His mentor's voice echoed in his mind. "Every trader faces moments like these, Aarya. It's easy to let excitement cloud your judgment. Always return to your principles. What does your strategy say?"

His principles. Aarya had crafted a strategy based on diversification, risk management, and emotional discipline. Each trade was meant to contribute to a larger plan, not detract from it. Yet here he was, staring at a single opportunity that threatened to derail everything he had built.

As the hours passed, Aarya found himself oscillating between excitement and fear. He confided in his close friends—traders who had witnessed his transformation and who understood the journey he had taken. They offered mixed perspectives, some urging him to go for it, while others advised caution.

"I'd say take the chance," said Vikram, his voice brimming with enthusiasm. "This is a huge opportunity! Imagine the returns if you're right. You've done your research, and if the product is a hit, it's going to change everything!"

"But what if it doesn't?" Aarya countered, feeling the tension rising. "What if I lose everything I've worked for?"

"It's a calculated risk, Aarya," Vikram said. "You can't let fear dictate your decisions. This could be your moment to shine."

Aarya appreciated Vikram's enthusiasm, but the weight of the potential gamble pressed heavily on his chest. As he settled into bed that night, sleep eluded him. He tossed and turned, his mind racing through scenarios, each one a vivid picture of either success or failure.

What if he went all in and lost? How would he face his mentor? His friends? He had worked so hard to establish himself as a disciplined trader, and this gamble could unravel all of it. But the thought of missing out on a once-in-a-lifetime opportunity felt equally suffocating.

The sun rose, casting a warm glow over the city, but Aarya felt a chill run down his spine as he brewed his morning coffee. Today would be the day he made the decision. As he sipped the rich brew, he opened his laptop and logged into his trading account. The market was about to open, and he had just a few moments to decide.

With the pre-market news buzzing in his ears, Aarya felt the familiar thrum of adrenaline surge through him. The stock was already trending upwards, and the excitement was palpable. He could feel the lure of the gamble drawing him closer, whispering promises of riches and validation.

But he knew he had to ground himself. He pulled up his trading journal, a testament to his journey and growth. Page after page documented his progress, the lessons learned from failures, the strategies he had developed over time. He flipped to the most recent entry, detailing the wisdom imparted by his mentor—wisdom that had kept him afloat through turbulent times.

As he read through his reflections, the panic that had gripped him began to ease. He remembered the principles he had embraced: diversification, risk management, emotional discipline. This moment was a test, a culmination of everything he had learned.

With a deep breath, Aarya decided it was time to take a step back. Instead of going all in, he would approach the opportunity with caution. He would allocate a portion of his capital to the trade, enough to participate in the potential upside but not so much that it would jeopardize his overall strategy.

He entered a modest order, one that reflected his belief in the opportunity while remaining true to his disciplined approach. As he clicked the "submit" button, a wave of relief washed over him. He had faced the ultimate gamble, and while he had chosen to take a risk, he had done so in a way that aligned with the trader he had become.

As the market opened, the stock surged. Aarya watched the numbers dance across his screen, his heart racing with excitement. But this time, there was no panic. He had made his decision, and no matter the outcome, he felt grounded in the knowledge that he had adhered to his principles.

In the days that followed, the product launch proved to be a resounding success. The stock price soared, climbing to heights that had once seemed like a distant dream. Aarya watched his modest investment grow, but more than the financial gains, he savoured the satisfaction of having made a decision that aligned with his journey.

The moment felt surreal; he had faced the lure of temptation and emerged stronger. It wasn't just about the profits; it was about the growth, the evolution from a trader who chased quick wins to one who understood the value of patience and discipline.

As Aarya celebrated his gains, he also reflected on the lessons learned through this process. He had come to appreciate that trading was not just about financial success but about personal growth and resilience. Each challenge had shaped him, each mistake had been a stepping stone toward understanding the market's unpredictable nature.

With the winds of change blowing in his favor, Aarya realized that this was not the end but rather a new beginning. He had found balance—a way to integrate ambition with caution, excitement with discipline. He knew there would always be new opportunities and new challenges, but now he was equipped with the tools to navigate them.

His mentor reached out to congratulate him, and Aarya shared the news of his recent success. "You did it, Aarya," his mentor said, a note of pride in his voice. "You've proven to yourself that you can face temptation and remain grounded. That's what separates successful traders from the rest."

As Aarya sat back in his chair, a smile crept across his face. The road ahead was still uncertain, but he was no longer the trader who succumbed to panic or temptation. He had become a calm, collected individual who understood the market's rhythm and could navigate its ebbs and flows.

The journey had transformed him, and with each trade, he embraced the lessons that came with it. He had emerged not just as a trader but as a resilient individual, ready to take on whatever challenges lay ahead. And in that realization, Aarya found peace—a calm within the storm, prepared for whatever the market had in store.

Chapter 15: The Everyday Legend

The sun had begun its slow descent over the horizon, casting a warm golden hue across the city. Aarya leaned against the balcony railing of his apartment, sipping a cup of freshly brewed coffee as he watched the world below. The hustle and bustle of life continued unabated, yet he felt a profound stillness within himself. It was a moment of reflection, a pause to consider how far he had come in his journey as a trader.

It had been weeks since his decisive trade—the gamble that had reinforced his growth and solidified his understanding of the market. The euphoria of success still lingered, but Aarya knew that this feeling was not simply about the money; it was about the journey that had led him here. He had weathered the storm of uncertainty, faced the temptation of quick riches, and emerged on the other side with hard-earned wisdom.

As he stood there, memories flooded back—of late nights spent poring over charts, of the thrill of executing a trade, and the bitter taste of failure that had once haunted him. He had started as a naïve dreamer, enticed by the idea of quick wealth, only to be humbled by the market's unpredictability. Each misstep had been a lesson, shaping his understanding and refining his approach.

In those early days, he had chased after every trend, convinced that the next big trade would make him rich overnight. But with each failure came a revelation: success in trading was not a sprint; it was a marathon. It required discipline, patience, and a strategic mindset. Aarya had learned to respect the market, to understand that it was as much about psychology as it was about numbers.

He recalled the support of his friends—Vikram, Priya, and the others—who had stood by him through thick and thin. They had celebrated his successes and commiserated with him during setbacks. Their camaraderie had been invaluable, reminding him that trading was not a solitary endeavor. The trading community was a tapestry of experiences, woven together by shared struggles and victories.

Now, as Aarya reflected on his journey, he realized that he had developed a trading philosophy rooted in purpose. No longer did he trade out of desperation or impulsiveness; he approached each decision with a clear strategy in mind. He set goals that aligned with his values, focusing not just on profits but on building a sustainable trading career.

Aarya had also begun to understand the importance of risk management. He recognized that every trade came with its own set of uncertainties, and he was now better equipped to navigate them. By diversifying his portfolio and employing stop-loss strategies, he had safeguarded his investments against unforeseen market fluctuations.

It wasn't merely about avoiding losses; it was about creating a trading environment that allowed him to thrive. He found joy in the process—the thrill of analyzing market trends, the satisfaction of executing a well-thought-out trade, and the peace that came with knowing he was in control of his financial future.

With this newfound clarity, Aarya felt a calling to share his experiences with others. He understood that many traders embarked on their journeys without the guidance he had received. They were often driven by dreams of wealth, only to find themselves lost in a sea of uncertainty.

He began to document his story, not just as a personal narrative but as a source of inspiration for everyday traders. He wanted to show them that trading was not merely about financial gain; it was about personal growth, resilience, and the relentless pursuit of knowledge.

Aarya established a blog, sharing his insights, lessons learned, and the strategies that had worked for him. He wrote about the psychological aspects of trading, emphasizing the importance of emotional discipline and the ability to weather the highs and lows of the market. His posts resonated with many, sparking discussions and fostering a sense of community among fellow traders.

As he engaged with his readers, Aarya realized that he had become a source of inspiration—a "legend" in the making, not because of his financial success, but because of the wisdom he imparted. He took great pride in helping others navigate their own journeys, providing them with the tools they needed to succeed.

Aarya's blog quickly gained traction, and he found himself interacting with a diverse community of traders—newbies, veterans, and everyone in between. Each person had their own unique story, their own challenges, and triumphs. They shared strategies, tips, and experiences, creating a vibrant ecosystem of learning and growth.

One evening, Aarya hosted a live webinar where he discussed his journey and the lessons learned along the way. He shared anecdotes from his trading experiences, emphasizing the importance of patience and discipline. As he spoke, he could see the engagement from his audience, their eyes reflecting a mix of hope and determination.

After the session, he received a flood of messages from participants, expressing gratitude for the insights he had shared. Many spoke of their own struggles and how his story had inspired them to approach trading with renewed purpose. In that moment, Aarya understood that he was not just a trader; he was a mentor, a guide, and a source of encouragement for those seeking to forge their own paths in the market.

Yet, despite his successes, Aarya remained grounded. He knew that the fight for success was ongoing, that the market would continue to present challenges. Each day was a new opportunity to learn, adapt, and grow. He no longer viewed trading as a means to an end;

it was a journey filled with lessons, each one contributing to his development as a trader and an individual.

With this understanding, Aarya approached his trading with a sense of humility. He realized that even the most seasoned traders faced setbacks, and that the key to long-term success lay in resilience and adaptability. The market was inherently unpredictable, but he was no longer afraid. He had learned to embrace the uncertainty, to navigate it with confidence.

He continued to refine his trading strategy, staying attuned to market trends and economic indicators. He sought out opportunities, but now he approached them with a sense of purpose rather than desperation. Each trade was a calculated decision, aligned with his overarching goals and values.

As Aarya's journey unfolded, he began to consider the legacy he wanted to leave behind. He envisioned a world where traders approached the market with a sense of responsibility, equipped with the knowledge and skills to navigate its complexities. He wanted to inspire a new generation of traders who understood that success was not just about profits, but about personal growth and resilience.

To further this vision, Aarya partnered with local organizations to conduct workshops and seminars for aspiring traders. He shared his experiences and knowledge, empowering others to approach trading with purpose and discipline. His workshops became a safe space for individuals to ask questions, share their fears, and learn from one another.

The impact of his efforts was profound. Aarya witnessed firsthand the transformation of many participants—individuals who had once felt lost in the world of trading, now gaining confidence and clarity. They began to view trading as a journey, not just a destination, and the sense of community they built fostered a supportive environment for learning.

As the weeks turned into months, Aarya found himself standing at a crossroads once again. The trading world was constantly evolving, and he understood that he needed to adapt to remain relevant. He sought out new strategies, embraced technology, and delved into the realm of algorithmic trading.

With each new challenge came a renewed sense of purpose. Aarya felt invigorated by the prospect of expanding his knowledge and skills, of exploring new avenues within the trading landscape. He remained committed to his principles while also remaining open to innovation.

The market, with all its unpredictability, continued to be a source of fascination for him. He approached it with a sense of curiosity, eager to uncover new insights and strategies that would propel him forward. Each day brought the promise of discovery, and Aarya embraced it wholeheartedly.

In the quiet moments of reflection, Aarya recognized that he had become more than just a trader; he had become an everyday legend. His story was one of resilience, determination, and growth—a testament to the power of learning from failure and the importance of discipline in achieving success.

As he gazed out at the city, Aarya felt a sense of gratitude wash over him. He was grateful for the challenges he had faced, for the lessons learned, and for the people who had supported him along the way. He understood that his journey was far from over; it was an ongoing adventure filled with opportunities for growth and discovery.

And in that realization, Aarya found peace. He had weathered the storms, embraced the uncertainty, and emerged as a trader with purpose. As he took a deep breath, he felt a renewed sense of determination. The market would continue to test him, but he was ready for whatever lay ahead.

In the end, Aarya had learned that success was not merely measured by financial gains, but by the wisdom gained along the way. He had transformed from a naïve dreamer into a seasoned trader, and his journey would continue to inspire others to embrace their own paths.

As he turned away from the balcony, a smile graced his face. The future was bright, and he was ready to embrace it—one trade at a time.

Dear Readers,

As I reach the end of this journey of sharing Aarya's story, I want to take a moment to express my heartfelt gratitude to each one of you. Writing this book has not only been a labor of love but also a profound learning experience for me. Aarya's evolution from a naïve dreamer to a seasoned trader mirrors the path many of us tread in our own lives, filled with challenges, setbacks, and triumphs.

When I first set out to pen this tale, my aim was to provide insight into the world of trading—not merely as a means to financial gain, but as a journey of personal growth, resilience, and discipline. Aarya's journey resonates with anyone who has ever dared to chase a dream, confront their fears, and learn from their mistakes. It serves as a reminder that the road to success is often fraught with obstacles, but with dedication and a commitment to learning, it is possible to rise above.

Through Aarya's experiences, I hoped to illustrate that success is not defined by the absence of failure, but rather by the ability to learn, adapt, and persevere. Each chapter reflects the struggles and victories that many of us face, and I believe that these lessons extend beyond the trading floor. They speak to the core of human experience, reminding us that we are all capable of growth, no matter our circumstances.

I am deeply grateful to my family, friends, and mentors who supported me throughout the writing process. Your encouragement and belief in my vision kept me motivated, and I hope to inspire others in the same way.

To my readers, I invite you to reflect on your own journeys. Embrace the lessons learned along the way, celebrate your successes, and don't be afraid to confront your fears. Remember that every challenge presents an opportunity for growth, and that even in the face of adversity, you have the strength to rise above.

Thank you for joining me on this journey through Aarya's world. I hope his story resonates with you and inspires you to pursue your own dreams with purpose and determination.

Here's to the everyday legends we all aspire to be.

Warm regards,

Anshumala Singh

Don't miss out!

Visit the website below and you can sign up to receive emails whenever Anshumala Singh publishes a new book. There's no charge and no obligation.

https://books2read.com/r/B-A-IYPWB-JQKBF

BOOKS 2 READ

Connecting independent readers to independent writers.

Did you love *The Everyday Trader - Trader's Fight for Success*? Then you should read *Illusion - The Veil*[1] by Anshumala Singh!

[2]

In an age where information flows incessantly and perceptions can be easily manipulated, the concept of reality has become increasingly elusive. Illusion is a narrative that aims to peel back the layers of deception that often cloud our understanding of the world. Through the intertwined lives of Clara and Ethan, I explore themes of truth, memory, and the human psyche, inviting readers to question the very nature of their realities.

I encourage you to reflect on your own experiences and beliefs. How often do we accept what is presented to us without questioning its validity? How do we navigate the complexities of our thoughts and emotions in a world that seems to thrive on chaos and uncertainty? It is

---

1. https://books2read.com/u/mZ8gwe

2. https://books2read.com/u/mZ8gwe

my hope that Illusion will spark these questions and encourage you to seek deeper truths within yourself.

This book is not just a tale of mystery and intrigue; it is a journey into the heart of what it means to be human in a world where the lines between reality and illusion blur. Thank you for taking the time to engage with this exploration, and may it resonate with you long after the last page is turned.